Misty

as she stepped into 1 door and it shut with ....k, making her jump. His home was the same as before, increasing her nervousness as she looked around. The picture of Scavenger floated behind her eyes, making her stare at the man with her.

I'll tell him I'm not ready and ask him to take me home. She turned to tell him and stopped. He looked so alone as he gazed at her, her resolve melted and the words died in her throat.

He took her hand. "Are you afraid of me?"

"No. Yes. I mean..."

"It's all right," he said as he laid his hands on her shoulders. He gave her a small smile. "You've been saving yourself, haven't you?"

She nodded, feeling her face grow hot.

He massaged her shoulders, helping her relax. "I'm as far from Mr. Right as you get, you know."

"I don't think so," she whispered.

"Say the word, and I'll take you home right now." He snorted. "If you knew the truth about me, you'd run for the hills."

Misty smiled as she laid her hands on his chest. "I don't know about that. I do know I want to be with you, right here, right now, whoever you are."

Praise for Annette Miller

"[*NIGHT ANGEL*] is the first book of Ms. Miller's *Angel Haven* series, and I am hoping she will come up with a bunch more."

Bedeviled Angel

by

Annette Miller

An Angel Haven Romance, Book 2

Bedeviled Angel

Cover Art by *Angela Anderson*

The Wild Rose Press, Inc.
PO Box 708
Adams Basin, NY 14410-0708
Visit us at www.thewildrosepress.com

Publishing History
First Faery Rose Edition, 2015
Print ISBN 978-1-62830-718-4
Digital ISBN 978-1-62830-719-1

An Angel Haven Romance, Book 2
Published in the United States of America

Dedication

For Brian, Scot, and Alex,
who always believed I could realize my dream.

Chapter One

Misty hobbled through the New York rush hour crowd, her pinched toes shrieking for mercy inside the Jimmy Choo's Rena insisted she wear.

"High heels ought to be outlawed," she grumbled. "No matter how good they look." *I don't know why I let Rena talk me into using this stupid pair. Just because she can wear these things doesn't mean everyone can.*

She checked her watch, staring in disbelief at the time. Late again. *If the public knew I was a hero, I could use my power to get there faster.*

"Excuse me."

Misty stopped and turned. Irritated at the delay, her breath caught in her throat. A man stood behind her, holding out one of her bags. He was at least six feet, five inches tall, his T-shirt pulled tight across his wide chest, outlining the muscles beneath. Her glance drifted downward to the jeans hugging his hips, the seams straining around his legs. She swallowed hard, wondering what he looked like under that dark blue denim.

She forced her gaze back to his face. Some of his red hair had escaped the ponytail he sported, and the eye-patch covering his left eye was not big enough to hide the scar starting at his hairline and ending in the middle of his cheek. Had his nose been broken? It looked like it. He could pass for an eighteenth century

1

pirate, she thought.

"You dropped this," he said, his slight British accent surprising her.

She reached out to take it, her fingers brushing his. "Thanks. I never knew it was gone."

"Where're you off to in such a hurry?"

"I'm meeting a friend for dinner, and I'm late." She sighed. "Again."

He smiled, taking some of the bags from her hands. "Why don't you drive?"

She pointed to her right. "The restaurant is just down there." She grinned. "I was going to walk then decided to run."

"Want some company?"

"Sure." She nodded. *It'd be worth being late now*, she thought.

He offered her his arm, and they headed toward the restaurant. "Taylor Tremain."

"Misty Severin," she said. "Thanks for the help."

"You're welcome." He turned serious. "I'm surprised I actually saw the bag fall. I'm not at my best currently."

Misty glanced at him. "Problems?"

He shrugged. "I'm job hunting and nobody's hiring."

"Do you have any prospects at all?" she asked, holding his arm a little tighter.

He shook his head. "A few, but not enough. Right now, I'm working nights as mall security. Between that and job hunting during the day, I guess I'm half asleep."

"Night work is hard on the body," she said. *And what a body it is.*

Someone called her name, and they turned simultaneously.

"We seem to be at your destination."

She nodded, gazing into his right eye. It was as blue as the Caribbean Sea. "Thanks for walking with me."

He hesitated, looking like he wanted to say more. "Would you meet me here for dinner tomorrow night around six?" he finally asked.

Misty's heart pounded in her chest. *Oh yeah. I'll be here with bells on.* But caution kept her quiet. What if he was some nut job or a serial killer? It'd kill her hero street cred to be found hacked to death by some lunatic. But his right eye was kind, and they'd be in public. Besides, she could take care of herself.

"Okay," she said. "Sounds great."

He raised her hand to his lips, kissing it lightly. "Until tomorrow."

Misty was still watching his retreating figure as her friend walked up.

"You've got another new boyfriend?" Rena asked. "You could've said something, you know." She raised her hands to stop Misty from saying anything. "I know I used to be the one with the revolving door of men, but you're catching up. I wouldn't have even told the rest of the team." She gave her friend a stern glare. "The honeymoon's over, isn't it?"

Misty rolled her eyes. "You know, Rena, it'd be nice if you let me get a word in edgewise." She stared at Taylor's retreating figure. "Actually, we just met."

Rena watched him walk away then grinned, nudging her with her elbow. "So is he another candidate for the list of 'Men Not Going to Heaven Because What

They Do to a Pair of Pants Is a Sin'?"

"Right now, he *is* the entire list. Come on. Let's order, and I'll tell you all about it."

****

Jack McClennan, the man calling himself Taylor Tremain, hurried down the street, limping the last few paces before stopping in front of a sleek, futuristic, black van. Glancing over his shoulder, he murmured, "Defensive systems off." The lock popped and the door opened with a soft hiss. He hauled himself into the driver's seat, and the door shut with a quiet click behind him.

He pulled off his right boot for the second time that day. "Engage autopilot. Enter coordinates for Warehouse One. Surveillance systems up. Let's go home."

As the auto-drive engaged, he grabbed a large briefcase from between the seats and opened it, revealing tools for slim wire and computer circuitry repair. He stretched his leg across the passenger seat and rolled up his pant leg. Peeling back the artificial skin, he popped open a panel the length of his shin. He shook his head, sighing when he saw the same wire had broken loose, again. It needed to be replaced.

"Bloody junk," he growled, soldering the wire as the van drove him home.

The bay door to the warehouse opened, closing silently when the van idled to a stop next to a beat up Chevy. He climbed out and limped to the living area. All he wanted to do was collapse on the sagging couch, but passed it, in favor of the bedroom and the small bathroom beyond.

Running water in the sink, he pulled off the eye-patch, placing it on the back of the toilet. He stared at the solid white artificial eye, lightly fingering the scar that ran down his face. His eye was just about the only part that didn't give him problems. Considering he'd ripped it out of an android, and it wasn't government-issue, it was to be expected. He wore the eye-patch for show. The scanners in the eye let him see perfectly all the time.

"They should've let me die," he whispered.

He stared at his reflection before pulling off his shirt, splashing water on his face, and rubbing his wet hands on the back of his neck. "Nice to meet you, Taylor Tremain." He shook his head. "Just bloody terrific. As if I don't have enough identities to keep track of, I come up with another one on the spur of the moment."

The water swirled down the drain, and he watched the droplets drip off his chin. Misty's face intruded on his thoughts and, against his better judgment, he let her. He'd lied to her right from the start. He lived on lies these days, but he hated them, hated himself for being reduced to using them.

He'd studied her when she'd taken her bag back. She was beautiful. Her round face gave her a youthful look, but the full lips were definitely a woman's. Her hair was soft brown, almost auburn, hanging halfway down her back, her eyes maybe a shade darker. He'd slowly looked her over, taking in the full breasts, the small waist, and those long, nicely shaped legs.

What had possessed him to ask her out? He shook his head. He remembered how Misty looked, the life and laughter in her eyes. Her touch on his arm had shocked him. The same vibrancy had drawn him to his wife the day they'd met years ago. Asking her out must've been a moment of insanity on his part, nothing more. One date wouldn't hurt, would it? He glanced at himself in the fogged glass of the old mirror.

"You're a liar and a fraud, hero." He sneered at his reflection. "You just keep telling yourself lying to her is for her own good, and maybe you'll believe it." He squeezed his eyes shut. If he wasn't careful, he'd end up as crazy as his ULTRA records indicated.

He snatched the towel from the hook on the wall. "If she knew the truth about me, she could get hurt, even killed, just like..." He threw the towel on the floor. *"Damn it!"*

Limping to what could loosely be called a kitchen, he snatched a beer from the compact fridge. He yanked out the rubber band, scratching the back of his head as his long hair fell around his shoulders. He hobbled to the living room, easing himself down on the couch, and stretched his leg out to rest on the coffee table. He turned on the TV, letting the news babble in the background while his mind wandered.

A name pulled him out of his reverie and he frowned. "Captain Starblast, leader of the hero team, the Challengers, will be dedicating the new children's wing of St. Anne's Memorial Hospital tomorrow at noon. As the premier hero team in the city, the Challengers not only defend the people who live here, but also help the community on a more personal level."

The other news anchor nodded. "That's right. The people know they can always count on the Challengers for any task, no matter how large or small."

"Damn heroes. At least one of us got something good out of my trial, captain," he snarled at the image.

He picked up the remote to turn off the TV when he heard his name.

"Who is the Scavenger? We'll be exploring that question tonight on NewsLine at ten. We'll have an exclusive interview with a prominent ULTRA psychologist. Tune in. It should be very informative."

"I've finally made the big time. Can't miss my television debut." He checked his watch, noting he still had a few hours to kill.

Glancing at his desk, he spied a note on top of a new stack of paperwork to replace the stack he'd finished the day before. He flipped it open and read:

Hey, Jack.

Call this pile an early Christmas present.

Ho, ho, ho!

Frank

He snatched the page off the top and began typing. "Bloody hell, I hate paperwork."

Chapter Two

At five minutes to ten, Jack grabbed a beer and settled back on the couch, clicking on the small lamp on the end table. He raised the volume, wanting to make sure he heard everything.

He frowned. "What have they discovered that's worth devoting their highest rated news show to me?"

The reporter sat behind a desk, her dark business suit a telling sign this was a serious matter. "Good evening and welcome to another edition of NewsLine. I'm Marla Cramp," she said. "Who is the Scavenger? Tonight, we'll answer that question. With me is Dr. George Fenmore from ULTRA, the United Law-enforcement Tactical Response Agency."

Jack stiffened. What the hell? Had he heard that right?

The camera pulled back, revealing more of the studio. "Dr. Fenmore and other criminal psychologists have been appointed by Commander Michael Frailer, to see if this dangerous man can be apprehended." She turned to the man next to her. "Good evening, Dr. Fenmore."

George Fenmore pulled at his tie, giving his hostess a nervous smile. "Good evening, Ms. Cramp."

Jack shot to his feet, shattering the beer bottle in a tightening grip. Liquid sprayed everywhere. Blood ran down his hand and the alcohol burned, but none of it mattered. If not for the man on the television, he and his friends wouldn't be in hiding, his wife would still be with him, and the past ten years wouldn't have been hell.

He stood there, staring at the screen. *"You bastard!"*

Jack still had trouble believing Fenmore had been his toughest rival at ULTRA. In the field, the armor swam on the thin man, making him look like a bookkeeper trying to be a soldier. Now, he was playing at being the nervous doctor, pulling at his tie, smoothing his perfect pants, fidgeting with his small, round glasses. Fenmore's strength and intelligence had always been underestimated, but Jack knew all about the little man. After all, they'd worked together for nearly six years.

He gave the image on the television screen a mock salute. "You're still one hell of an actor, George. My congratulations."

Marla folded her hands on the desk. "Let's start by telling the viewers a little more about ULTRA."

George cleared his throat. "ULTRA is one of the larger agencies for dealing with paranormal crime, threats to the world, and terrorists. We headquarter here in New York but have other facilities across the country. We work in concert with other world agencies in dealing with the previously mentioned threats. We're basically the equivalent of INTERPOL for paranormal crimes. Our current commander is Michael Frailer. He's done very well ever since he took office five years ago."

Marla nodded and made some notes before diving right into the heart of the story. "Dr. Fenmore, your group has uncovered information recently about Scavenger, one of the top ten villains in the city. Can you enlighten us?"

Fenmore settled back in the chair. "We believe Scavenger is the former ULTRA field commander by the name of Jack McClennan. I worked with him when ULTRA was still new. Because of my past experience with him, Commander Frailer has asked for my help." He paused for moment, his eyes sad. "He was the best agent the organization ever had."

Jack paced in front of the couch, glaring at the television. "Finally got around to revealing my name to the public. It's about bloody time. It only took you a decade."

Marla tapped a pencil on the desk. "What supporting evidence do you have?"

Fenmore folded his hands in his lap, sitting up a little straighter. "Thirteen years ago, we discovered someone inside the organization was selling secrets and arms. McClennan's wife contacted us and turned him in. Because of her information, he was convicted of treason and dealing black market arms." Fenmore paused. "And her murder."

"He killed her?"

Fenmore nodded slowly. "I'm afraid so. She never had a chance." He stared directly into the camera almost as if Fenmore knew Jack would be watching.

"The little weasel's trying to make me look worse than I really do," he growled.

Fenmore cleared his throat. "When the prisoners found out he was a former law enforcement agent, he was in constant altercations. One night he was beaten so badly, it was thought he wouldn't survive."

She nodded. "What steps were taken to save his life?"

Fenmore leaned forward, laying his arm on the desk. "I suggested he be used for experimental cybernetics. If he died, nothing was lost. If he lived, it would be a huge step toward helping other, more deserving people, and he could serve the rest of his sentence at ULTRA's prison facility, HighPower." He smiled a little. "McClennan and I were friends. I wanted to help him."

"Oh, yeah, George," Jack said. "We were great friends. We were about as close as rival baseball fans."

Fenmore nodded his head. "Some at ULTRA felt McClennan should've received the death penalty."

Marla sat forward, a gleam of anticipation in her eyes. "Why didn't he?"

"His service record," he said simply. "It gave him life in prison instead of death. As a top agent, he'd made some powerful friends."

She nodded. "Please continue."

Fenmore adjusted his glasses. "The surgery was hard on McClennan, physically. His body rejected the implants, putting him in a coma that lasted several months. When he woke, his former supervisor was there, watching over him. He lashed out, screaming about betrayal, and broke the man's neck."

"He certainly does a lot of killing, doesn't he?" Marla said.

Fenmore nodded, a small smile on his lips. "He escaped and we at ULTRA noticed a set of field armor missing."

"It wasn't just any armor!" Jack shouted at the images, his hands curling. "It was mine!"

Fenmore continued looking into the camera. "When reports started coming in about heroes and villains missing weaponry, we knew McClennan was putting together his own power base to take revenge. I've been working with Commander Frailer to try to bring him to justice."

"Pretty words, George." Jack sneered. "How long did you have to practice to say them without choking?"

Fenmore moved his chair slightly to his left. "Here's a picture of what he looked like thirteen years ago. He's excellent at disguise, so he may have radically altered his appearance, we're not sure."

The picture behind them showed a man with shoulder length red hair, sharp blue eyes, and a lopsided grin. The green ULTRA armor gleamed brightly in the photo, the pride on his face almost cocky.

Marla turned to the camera. "If anyone has any information at all, please call the number at the bottom of the screen." She looked off camera. "Someone's already calling? Excellent."

Jack snatched the disposable cell phone off his desk and dialed the station. "I want to speak to Fenmore," he growled.

He waited while they set up a line in the studio, seeing his past flash in his mind. His wife lying in a pool of blood, her black hair sticky with it as he held her. The beating in prison where he'd been cornered, and how the guards had turned their backs. Finally, the escape from the hospital, and all the long years on the run.

"If you wanted to get my attention, Fenmore, it worked."

"Jack, it's been a long time," he said, his voice

about as soothing as sandpaper. "How can I help you?"

"You know how," Jack growled.

Fenmore smiled as he shook his head. "You need to turn yourself in. I can't help you unless you let me."

Jack laughed. "I know about your plans for me. Now let me tell you something, George. Someday I'll find you and whoever you answer to. Next time I see you, you're dead."

"I'm sorry you feel that way. I'd hoped you'd still consider me a friend."

Jack threw the phone against the wall, sick of Fenmore's nasal voice. He grabbed the pistol on his desk and shot the television screen dead center, and threw the gun at the smoking wreck. "Go to hell!"

He yanked open the top drawer and pulled out a creased photograph, the corners dog-eared, the frame missing. A beautiful, black-haired woman smiled at him. He traced her face with his finger, pushing down the grief threatening to consume him every time he looked at her.

"Carol," he murmured. "I miss you, sweetheart. I wish you were here." He walked back to the couch and slowly sat down. Running a hand through his hair, he closed his eyes and hung his head. "When did everything get so hard?"

****

"It's five o'clock, and I don't have a damn thing to wear!" Misty's shout was muffled as it drifted to Rena from inside her walk-in closet. Throwing her hand up, she stopped Misty's clothes in mid-air as her friend chucked clothes out, grateful again for her telekinesis. "Everything in here sucks!"

Rena looked at the growing pile on the floor.

"What's the matter, kid? Nervous?"

Misty stuck her head out. "The last time I was this nervous on a date was my junior prom."

Rena stepped over Misty's clothes. "Everything turned out fine for that, right?"

"No. I threw up all over him."

Rena cringed, trying to hide her grin. "Ouch. Not good."

"I saw that sneaky smile, Red," Misty said, scowling. "Watch it."

Using her telekinesis, Rena grabbed Misty and sat her firmly on the bed. She marched into the closet, pulling out black dress slacks, a white blouse, and a black vest. "Wear this and your black pumps," she said. "That way, when you're running for the bathroom, you won't fall off your heels."

Misty quickly changed and checked herself out in the full-length mirror. "I look good. You're a genius."

Rena chewed her bottom lip. "I'll send you my bill."

Misty glanced at her. "I know that look. What are you upset about?"

"I'm not upset," Rena said, folding her arms and taking a step back.

"Yes, you are. The only time you chew your lip is when you're worried. Spill it."

"Oh. Last night after you fell asleep on the couch, there was a news special on the Scavenger." She telepathically showed Misty the broadcast from the night before.

Misty brushed her hair. "Okay, so ULTRA's got their knickers in a twist. How's that different from any other day?"

"Don't you think their Jack McClennan looks a lot like your Taylor Tremain?"

Misty quickly applied makeup. "A little, I guess." She turned to Rena. "You aren't getting all motherly and paranoid in your old age, are you?"

"I don't know," Rena mumbled, looking at the floor.

Misty patted her arm. "I've got a few surprises of my own if he tries anything. Trust me."

Rena nodded. "Call if you need me."

"I will." She paused, flashing a grin. "Mom." Using her desolidification powers, Misty slipped through the floor like a ghost.

Chapter Three

The Angel Haven limousine stopped a short distance from Misty's meeting place with Taylor. She saw him leaning against the building, looking up and down the street. He was dressed simply, just jeans, a plain white T-shirt, and a pair of work boots, badly scuffed. He'd pulled his hair back into a ponytail again, and the eye-patch was in place over his left eye. The glow of the setting sun turned the red in his hair to fire.

She stepped out of the car, waving as she headed toward him. "I hope I didn't keep you waiting long."

He pulled her arm through his. "Not at all. You look lovely." He grinned at her. "No running tonight?"

She shook her head. "Tonight I had the car. And you look pretty terrific yourself." She inwardly winced. *I sound like an idiot.* "So, where to?"

He gestured down the street. "Just down here. It's one of my favorites."

She smiled as he took her hand. "Sounds great."

There was no restaurant, only a hot dog vendor with a bright red and blue cart with enticing, steamy aromas drifting from it. Taylor waved to the man at the stand, getting a greeting in return as he led her over.

"Good evening, Frank. Two for dinner, please." He stood there, his back ramrod straight, the tone in his voice a bit snobbish.

Misty looked at Frank. He could've been anywhere

from his early forties to his late fifties. He had a little pot belly, and his brown hair was scattered with gray, looking like it had never been touched with a brush. Lines crinkled at the corners of his eyes as he broke out in a broad smile.

"Hey, Taylor," he said, rolling his eyes when Taylor raised one imperious eyebrow. He sighed. "Oh, all right. What'll it be, your Lordship?"

Taylor gave him a quick nod. "Two of your best, and spare no expense. Tonight, money is no object."

Frank winked at Misty. "Considering you got a tab about as long as the Bill of Rights, why should tonight be any different?" He opened the little door on top and Misty inhaled deeply.

"Those smell heavenly," she sighed.

Frank added almost everything he had on the cart to the two large hot dogs. They walked to a nearby bus bench and Misty sat down, placing their dinner next to her.

"I'll be right back," Taylor said. "I've got to get napkins and our drinks.

Misty loved the way his body moved when he walked. She watched the two men glance over their shoulders and Taylor frowned. *What could they be talking about?*

****

"Did you see the news last night?"

Frank nodded. "Sure did." He passed napkins, two sodas, and extra ketchup and mustard packs to his friend. "I knew you'd be concerned, so I sent out part of the team to gather information. We've got people at his house, his office, and his usual haunts."

"How the hell did Fenmore, of all people, get by

us?" Jack's good eye narrowed. "You told me all the conspirators were nailed. You said you did the body count yourself."

Frank wiped the top of the cart and frowned. "Don't give me that look, buddy. I taught you that look. All the bodies were accounted for that night."

Jack's hand curled into a tight fist, crushing the napkins. "Didn't anyone bother to check ID's?"

"After all these years, now you're beginning to doubt me?" Frank fiddled with some of the items on the cart. "All we can figure is the Council must've faked up some of their own people so the ID's would match."

Jack's shoulders sagged. "I'm sorry, Frank. You're my team leader for a reason. Send me everything you find."

Frank nodded. "Will do. I know how much you love paperwork. Now get back to your lady before she comes to find out what's keeping 'Taylor'."

****

Misty watched the men talk and grew worried. The looks on their faces would've scared the devil himself. She rubbed the back of her neck. That's it, she thought. No more beating up bad guys for a bit. I'm getting way too suspicious.

Taylor walked toward her, the dark look he'd had before replaced by a smile.

"What a killer smile," she murmured.

He sat next to her, placing a napkin on her knee. "Thank you."

She swallowed hard. "You heard me?"

He nodded. "You looked deep in thought for a moment. Was it my 'killer smile' that had you thinking, or merely the food?"

Feeling heat rising in her face, she stammered, "I was thinking what an unusual dinner date this is. I've got a friend from a very upscale, very proper family who wouldn't be caught dead eating hot dogs on a bus bench. Heck. She wouldn't be caught eating a hot dog."

He gave her a sly smile. "You want me to bring her down to earth for you? I'd be more than happy to oblige."

Misty's hand flew to her chest. "Heaven's, no. You may decide you like her more than me, and I'd never see the two of you again."

He hesitated a moment before reaching out and running a finger lightly down her cheek. "I don't think that's possible."

Misty gazed at him, her breath coming quicker as he didn't break eye contact. A car horn blew and she jumped, sticking her thumb in mustard. She looked away eating in silence, and when they finished, he threw away their trash and pulled her arm through his. They strolled down the street, enjoying the last of the cool spring air.

"You know what I'm currently doing to make a living," he said, watching the people passing on the way to their own destinations. "What about you?"

"I'm an attorney," she said.

He glanced at her. "An attorney? How many cases have you won?"

She laughed. "I'm a corporate attorney. All I do is draw up contracts and sit through boring merger talks." She gazed at him. "It's not as glamorous as people think."

"You don't take care of lawsuits and things like that?"

"Not any more. You can only listen to people whine for so long before it gets to you." She drew herself up. "I'm an official pencil pusher now."

"What did your family think of that?" He took her hand. "Just moving along?"

Misty hesitated. "Both of my parents are dead. They were killed when I was a child, and I have no brothers or sisters. My guardian supported me and told me to do whatever made me happy."

He squeezed her hand. "He sounds like a wise man."

Misty smiled. "My guardian was a close friend of my parents. He helped me through the tough time after their deaths. He took me into Angel Haven and raised me. His daughter, Kristin, is my age and she's the closest thing I have to a sister." *I think I'll leave out the desolidification powers, the hero team thing, and the beating up villains for now.*

"What's Angel Haven?"

She smiled. "That's the name he gave his home. He says it's a haven for his friends to forget their troubles when they need it. The house and grounds are pretty big. One of my housemates says it should be called Angel Heaven because it's almost that large."

What she didn't tell him was that Angel Haven was the base for her hero team, the Angels. Her guardian had taken in teens who also manifested paranormal abilities and had no place to go to learn to control them. In addition to having his own powers, the doctor was also a geneticist. He used his knowledge and ability to help Misty and her friends learn to use their powers. Her home truly *was* a haven for the Angels.

"Really? And how many housemates do you

have?"

"Six. Most of them came in their teens. They were the children of my guardian's friends and their parents felt the kids would get a better education with him then in traditional schools."

"So Angel Haven is basically a very private, exclusive school."

She nodded. "It used to be. None of us are in school anymore, but we still live there for now. Kristin is supposed to be getting married, but her fiancé keeps putting it off. She thinks he might be having second thoughts."

Taylor tensed under her arm, and she looked at him. "Is something wrong?"

"My wife died thirteen years ago," he said in a low voice. "I still miss her, and it creeps up on me when I least expect it."

The pain in his voice brought tears to her eyes, and she blinked furiously. "Oh, Taylor, I'm so sorry."

He glanced down at her, smiling as he wiped her tears away. "Now I've upset you when we were having such a good time. Hey, how about a balloon?" He led her over to a man with a handful of brightly colored balloons.

She pulled the string of a hot pink one with a smiley face. She grinned. "This one works."

As they walked along, Misty watched Taylor continuously check over his shoulder. The nearly full moon rose, and the stars came out, dotting the sky with pinpricks of light. He checked the surrounding area more frequently the later it became.

"It's getting late," he said. "Is your ride coming to get you, or should I take you home?"

Misty picked at the balloon string. "I wasn't sure what time to tell him to come for me. You can take me home, if you want."

"Oh, I want." He tucked her hair behind her ear. "I want to take you home, very much."

He just stood there, gazing at her and she leaned fractionally closer. He broke contact first and walked her down the street to a four door Chevy with fading blue paint. A large dent over the right wheel well was beginning to rust along the edges. The interior wasn't much better. The black leather on the edges of the seats had cracked and the dashboard was dull and dirty.

He opened the door and frowned. "Hang on a second."

He leaned in and threw papers, CD cases, small boxes, and things she decided only men have in their cars into the backseat. As she saw how snugly his jeans hugged his butt, heat rose to her face.

If I died right now, I'd be happy, she thought. He is *so* on The List.

****

Misty directed him up the long driveway to the front of Angel Haven mansion. Tall columns stood the length of the low porch that went from one end of the house to the other. A single light glowed over the double doors.

"*This* is Angel Haven?"

"Home sweet home."

Taylor stepped out, opening her door for her. "I can't tell you all the times I've driven by here. I've always been impressed by this place." He paused. "Would you mind going out with a pauper again?"

She grinned at him as they headed for the front

door. "Are you making fun of me?"

He shook his head. "I wouldn't do something like that." He stepped closer to her and leaned in, just a little. He closed his eyes for a moment, pulling back when he opened them. "How about this Saturday?"

"Great. Same time, same place?"

"Sounds like a plan." He walked her to the door and turned her to face him.

"Thanks again for a wonderful night," she said, her voice barely a whisper.

Taylor reached out, stroking her cheek. "You're welcome."

She gazed at his face as he moved closer to her, too many emotions flashing through his one good eye. *This is it.*

He hesitated, finally stepping back from her. "Good night, Misty."

She couldn't believe he walked away.

Chapter Four

"Well, of course he didn't kiss you," Rena said, choking back her laughter. "You two just met."

Misty scowled. "As a telepath, you should be more sympathetic to my distress."

"You've got me confused with an empath. They're much better in the sympathy department." They jogged up the main stairs and into Rena's room. "As a telepath, I know you wanted to kiss him, not the other way around."

"Don't you dare laugh. I know he wanted to kiss me," she insisted. "But nothing. Not even a handshake."

Rena flopped on her bed. "Maybe he wants to take it slow. After all, he did ask you out again. Before you know it, you'll be ripping each other's clothes off."

She threw one of Rena's small stuffed animals at her. "You're impossible to talk to when you get like this, you know that?"

"What's the matter?" Rena cocked an eyebrow. "Jealous?"

Misty laughed. "Not hardly."

Rena sat up, crossing her legs. "So what's he like? All I've heard about is you, and I kind of know that story."

Misty sat at Rena's desk, rocking the chair back on two legs. "He didn't talk much about himself. He just asked about me."

"You're kidding, right? This guy *is* a gem," Rena muttered.

"All I really know is that he's looking for a job, he has a friend named Frank, and his wife died thirteen years ago." Misty shrugged. "That's about it."

Rena shook her head. "Too weird. Are you sure he's not the guy ULTRA's after?"

Misty headed for the door. "I'm not discussing that tonight." She waved over her head as she left. "See you tomorrow, Red."

****

Misty tossed and turned in her bed, picturing Taylor in her mind and reliving their first date. Every time he touched her, she felt she'd turn into a puddle right then and there. Rena was right. She'd wanted him to kiss her, or try something more intimate, but he'd been the perfect gentleman all evening.

She could still see his right eye, the azure blue a perfect complement to his fiery red hair. His hands had been so gentle every time he touched her. What would it feel like to have him touch her all over? She turned on her other side, punching her pillow. Thoughts like that were going to make it a long night.

****

The afternoon sun was warming up the day quickly as Jack drove to where he was supposed to pick up Frank. Drumming his fingers on the steering wheel as he sat at a red light, a familiar face pushed her way to the front of his mind. Misty hadn't left his thoughts since he'd taken her out. It was a good thing he remembered to tell Frank about the new identity he'd created before they'd met him.

Jack's eyes scanned the people walking and those

in the cars around him. The scanners in his eye let him see right through the patch like it wasn't there. The eye-patch was in place as usual when he was out in public. He didn't need it. He used it to stop too many questioning looks, too many raised eyebrows. He stared at the people again. Who was the most likely one out to get him? The woman walking the dog? The guy on his cell phone? He shook his head, tired of suspecting every person walking the face of the earth.

Movement to his left caught his attention, and he turned. Fenmore was heading into a small cafe with some other people in suits. Jack looked for a parking space, but found no open spots. As he watched his enemy laugh at something one of the men with him said, Jack's hands shook

He sat there staring until blaring horns made him move. Turning a corner, he saw Frank wave to him, and he pulled over. He decided against telling his friend that he just saw Fenmore. After all, it wouldn't do any good, and they'd probably end up doing something stupid.

Frank climbed in and Jack looked at him as they pulled away. "Got anything for me, yet?"

He shook his head. "Not much, right now." He flipped through a small pad. "Fenmore leaves the house around seven in the morning with a couple of ULTRA security guards. He has morning meetings with the ULTRA commander. He lunches at the better restaurants and when he's with others, he always treats."

Jack frowned. If Fenmore could afford the better places in town, why would he go into such a lower end cafe? "He can't be making that much at ULTRA. Can he afford it?" Something was wrong with the whole scenario.

"Oh, yeah," Frank said, nodding his head. "I had Amy poke his bank account. He can afford it. He and his wife both lead an extravagant lifestyle."

"Probably lets out the wife if we need help to take him down."

Frank nodded and turned to stare out the window. "We just need a little more time."

"Time," Jack said with a small laugh. "We've been running scared for more than a decade, and now ULTRA is pushing to wrap it all up. I don't think we have any more time."

He closed his eyes, seeing his painful past, and the friends he'd lost over the years. "Why didn't I leave it alone? None of this would've happened if I'd just ignored what Fenmore and his crowd were doing like I'd been warned."

"You couldn't. None of us could," Frank said, his voice hard. "Even if you did, Carol would've pursued it. You know she would've."

Jack hesitated and then nodded slowly. "I know. But I should've planned better, thought things through more." He snorted. "Now Fenmore's out there acting the good public servant, and I'm still locked in as the bad guy." He glanced at Frank. "Some world, huh?"

"So, tell the truth," Frank insisted. "You know the evidence. Make a statement to the press."

Jack's shoulders sagged as he stared at the traffic ahead of him. "I'm tired of this same conversation, Frank. I won't be believed."

Frank turned to him. "You think I'm not tired of saying the same thing, trying to get you to see reason? You always took chances before. Take one now and go public with what you learned at the beginning of this disaster. It may place a few doubts."

"I know," Jack said. "I'd like to see what kind of information we get before making any kind of move, if that's okay with you?"

"That'll do."

"Anything else?"

"Not now, but I'll be in touch." Frank watched his friend closely. "I didn't know you were dating again. How long have you known her?"

Jack squirmed in his seat. "We just met."

"Please tell me it was just the one date."

"We're going out again on Saturday," he mumbled.

"Maybe you should take it easy."

Jack sighed. "It's two dates." He pulled up to the curb.

Frank grabbed the door handle. "Someone's always watching you. I don't want to add her to our list of casualties."

"You think I don't know that?" he said, his voice raising. "Damn it, I'm tired of being alone. There's nothing serious between us. I just want to be with someone who doesn't know anything about me for a while."

Frank got out and leaned on the door before Jack pulled away. "At least go armed. It'll make me feel better."

Jack nodded. "Yes, Mother."

****

Jack drove back to where he'd seen Fenmore. Using the scanners in his left eye, he studied the cafe and saw Fenmore still inside. He waited until a space opened up and pulled in to wait for the man to come out. He looked at his watch. It looked like they'd just gotten their food so he had some time to kill.

He pulled out a small, digital camera from under the passenger seat. It wasn't the greatest quality, but he could at least get pictures to his people and see if anyone knew the men with Fenmore. He got out and found a spot that wouldn't be too conspicuous where he could take a few good shots.

Jack just got himself settled when they appeared. He quickly snapped off a few shots and tucked the small camera into his pants pocket. The others left and Fenmore stood there alone while his bodyguards brought his car around. Jack couldn't resist and stalked his way toward his nemesis.

"Hello, George," he growled. "What brings you down to my neighborhood?"

Fenmore jumped and jerked his head around. "Jack!" He took a deep breath and the smarmy smile was back. "I had meetings with some friends of mine. They seemed to think this place had good food."

Jack stepped closer to him. "And does it?"

"It's passable. I couldn't eat here on a daily basis, but it's a nice change." Fenmore looked him over. "I didn't think you knew how to come out in daylight anymore. You're paler than you used to be."

"I'm out and about more than you think. You know, I could get rid of you right here and now, and if I didn't need you alive, you'd be the top story on the six o'clock news."

"Too bad you don't have the guts to do what it takes," Fenmore said. "If you were smart enough, you wouldn't need me alive to get what you want." He nodded toward his car. "And now, you've lost your chance." He leaned close to Jack. "You're pathetic, McClennan."

Jack stood there while Fenmore got in the car and was driven away. He hung his head on the way back to his van. He really was pathetic. If he was going to conclude this situation in his favor, he needed to dig up the cold-hearted killer—the one he'd summoned from inside himself so many times before—and let him loose.

Jack started the engine and headed home.

Chapter Five

Misty yanked the brush through her hair. "This has been the slowest week of my life."

"Seeing your mystery man again?" Rena grinned. "And no wardrobe advice this time. I guess you're not as nervous?"

"Yes, I am and no, I'm not."

Rena watched her finish getting ready. "Ha!" She pointed. "You *are* nervous. Your hands are shaking."

"I am not, I tell you." Misty turned, staring at her. "It's anticipation." She passed through the floor, and Rena ran down the steps, meeting her at the front door.

"You need to quit doing that when you're done talking."

"But then, how would you get your exercise?" Misty grinned.

"When I think of a comeback for that, you're in big trouble!" Rena shouted as Misty hurried out to her sports car and drove away.

****

When Misty pulled up next to the curb in front of Taylor, he opened the door and frowned at the tiny interior.

Pointing to the small seats and almost nonexistent legroom, he grimaced. "You want me to fit in that?"

She grinned. "You can make it." She waited while he squeezed his large frame into the small bucket seat, reaching down to put it all the way back. He sighed as he put the seat belt on.

"See?" she said. "I told you. Now, how would you like to see how the other half lives?"

"I'd love to," he said, still adjusting himself to get comfortable in the tiny car. "What did you have in mind? Dinner with the Hiltons then off to England to visit with the Royals?"

She laughed. "Nothing so elaborate. How about dinner at one of my favorite restaurants then maybe a movie?"

The corners of his mouth twitched. "I suppose it'll do. But I thought I was paying for this date since I did the asking."

"Nope. Tonight, everything's on me."

His smile broke out fully. "I like you modern women. Can I borrow five bucks for gas?"

She turned sharply, his smile catching her off guard. *God help me if he really turns on the charm.* "What?"

"I'm kidding."

"Oh," she said, not sure if he was kidding or not.

They stood at the dining room entrance and Misty greeted some of the servers. She looked around, taking in how the deep burgundy carpet glowed under the golden lights from the chandelier and the diners speaking in hushed tones. This is how a restaurant should be, she thought.

The host rushed over. "Ms. Severin, it's a pleasure to see you again."

She smiled as she shook his hand. "Same here. I made sure to make reservations tonight instead of just dropping in."

He smiled. "Your usual table will be ready in a moment."

"You're just too good to me." She watched him hurry away.

"Do you own this place?" Taylor asked her.

She shook her head. "No. Just a lot of patronage on my part. You can't beat good service and excellent food."

They were shown to their table, and Misty looked up from her menu to see Taylor staring at her. "What?"

"I'd like to cook for you one night, if you'd like."

Warmth spread through her at his suggestion. "Sounds great." She bet she'd get a whole different service than what she got here. At least, she hoped she would.

They ordered and Misty asked for a bottle of her favorite wine. She kept glancing at him while they waited for their food and then while they ate. He caught her staring at him and smiled, reaching over to hold her hand.

The waiters cleared their table and Taylor looked at his watch as Misty settled the check. "It's almost eight thirty. We've been here over two hours."

She watched him. *Everything he does is sexy.* "Really? The next features for the movies don't start until after ten. How about a walk instead?"

"Perfect."

They strolled in the early June evening, the temperature still not too warm. As they walked, Misty noticed him again, constantly checking over his shoulder.

"What's wrong?"

"I'm not sure," he said. "I think we're being

followed."

She frowned as he glanced over his shoulder again. "Get down," he barked, pushing her behind a large planter near a storefront as a shot whizzed over their heads.

He glowered in the direction of the shot then turned to her. "Stay here and keep out of sight. I'll be back soon."

Misty watched as he sprinted down the street. Her power kicked in instinctively, and her left arm had faded halfway in the sidewalk to stop her from being injured. What the heck was going on she wondered. She pulled herself together, climbing to her feet with the rest of the crowd.

She smiled as people went about their business like nothing happened. With the rise in the number of paranormals, a gunshot wasn't nearly as frightening as someone shooting lasers from their hands, changing the weather, or conjuring huge alien weapons from thin air. *Ah, life in a city populated with paranormals*. She moved to a doorway to wait.

****

"Bloody hell," Jack muttered. "Doesn't he have anything else to do with his time?"

He ran around the corner, barely getting his arm up to block the large metal fist aiming at his head.

"Cyber-X," he said flatly. "You need a new hobby."

The metal arm and legs looked out of place on the middle-aged man with the military haircut and goggles perched on top of his head. The light blue, thickly padded leather vest creaked as the mercenary rested a wicked looking rifle on his hip.

"That would mean not fulfilling my contract. The contract is to bring in one ULTRA Field Commander Jack McClennan. That would be you." Cyber-X watched him closely. "And I've never left a job unfinished."

Jack rolled his shoulders, loosening the tenseness building. "What if I bought my contract? I can pay you ten times what it's worth."

Cyber-X shook his head, looking bored by the offer. "No, I don't think so. You see, you're the closest person that's ever come to being my equal. It's not about the money any more. It's about who's the better cyborg."

"You have a partner and that gives you the advantage. I'm alone."

Cyber-X shrugged. "She's my ace, and as I've been hunting you for six months and you're still free, I'm guessing you don't really need a partner."

Jack frowned. Six months? He needed to start keeping better track of the time. He didn't realize the cybernetic mercenary had been hunting him that long. "Then let it go. I'm taking up way too much of your time."

"Sorry," he said, shaking his head. "ULTRA wants you back. You've got a lot to answer for."

Jack drew the gun he'd concealed under his shirt. "Then you'd better plan on killing me, because that's the only way I'm going."

He jerked back as Cyber-X quickly drew a small, double-bladed knife and swung in a wide arc. He felt the familiar burn as the blade sliced his face open. He grabbed the mercenary's wrist and flipped him over his shoulder before he could take another swipe.

Blood ran down his face, dripping on his shirt. Jack's lip curled as anger raged through him. He cocked the gun. "Stay away from me, or I swear I'll kill you where you stand."

He fired off several rounds in quick succession, forcing Cyber-X to dive for cover. Jack ran back the way he came, slowing to a walk as he drew closer to Misty. He shook his head. "Leaving an enemy alive now?" he mumbled. "You're getting soft, hero."

Ignoring the looks people gave him, his mouth set in a grim line, he stomped down the sidewalk. He'll never stop, he thought. Not until he's completed his contract. He could admire determination in others, but in Cyber-X, it was getting downright annoying.

****

Misty waited, looking for Taylor. Why would someone shoot at him? Of course, they could've been aiming at her. As a member of the Angels' hero team and an ULTRA liaison, she always had some nutcase after her. It was only a matter of time before she was caught in her civilian identity.

She checked for him again. Still no Taylor. She started walking in the direction he'd gone. He could be hurt. Her desolidification powers would keep her safe from whoever it was, but then how would she keep that secret from him? She sighed. *Sometimes life is way too complicated.*

When she saw him coming, her eyes widened at his face. A bloody line ran from his forehead down the right side of his nose before tapering off near his chin. "What happened to you? Is that cut from a knife?"

He ignored her, brushing aside her concern. "Can I get a rain check for the rest of tonight?"

She nodded. "Sure. Is there anything I can do?"

He wiped blood out of his good eye. "I need a ride back to my place."

"All right." She paused, "Do you want to go to the police?" She unlocked the doors and they climbed in.

He wouldn't look at her. "It's all right. Just a case of mistaken identity, nothing more."

"Do you want to see a doctor?" She glanced at him. "It looks kind of deep."

A muscle jumped in his cheek, and he clenched his fists. "Leave it be!" he said, his voice rising. "I'm fine."

Misty opened her mouth several times to say something, anything to lighten the tension in the small car, but his mood darkened with every mile, and the only words he barked were directions to his apartment.

The building she pulled up to was neat, but years of weather had faded the paint, some of it peeling in places, and tufts of grass in the parking lot won the battle with the asphalt's cracks. Taylor got out without waiting for her and headed for the main entrance.

"Do you want some help?" she asked hesitantly, following him through the door and down the hall.

He threw open the door with a bang. "If you want," he grumbled, tossing his keys on the small armchair. Without a word, he headed for the kitchen.

Misty slid her blazer off as she looked around his home. No pictures, no keepsakes, or knickknacks—nothing personal at all. The air was stale and a layer of dust covered everything. She shivered with what Rena called the heebie jeebies. *What am I doing here? I don't know anything about him.* She flinched as she heard him banging in the kitchen.

"Do you want something to drink?" he yelled.

She walked to the doorway seeing anger still evident in his expression. "No, thanks." He wasn't angry at her, but she felt sorry for whoever it was.

He reached into the refrigerator, pulled out a beer, popped the cap off with his thumb, and took a long swallow.

"Do you have anything to clean up that cut?"

He jerked his head toward the small hallway. "There's stuff in the bathroom. Don't worry, though. I've been hurt worse than this."

She laid her hand on his arm. "Please, let me help you."

He stared at the bottle in his hand. "I haven't been very kind to you, have I?" He turned to her and smiled. "All right, if it'll make you feel better, you can play doctor."

Once in the bathroom, she grabbed the items she needed to clean up his face, then she felt the familiar nudging of a telepathic contact. *"What is it, Rena?"*

"I read your distress earlier. You okay?"

"Hunky dory." She couldn't stop herself from sighing. *"You worry too much. Taylor had a little mishap, that's all. I'm going to make sure he's okay then I'll be home."*

"Okay," Rena answered slowly. *"Take care."*

"All the time."

She returned to the living room, slowing when she heard him shouting at someone on the phone.

"I don't care how you do it. Get him off my back." He paused. "No, I don't know who issued it. If I took the time to do that, it'd be a death warrant, not just an arrest warrant." Another pause. "I don't care who authorized it. Bloody hell, Amy, just do it!"

He banged the phone down back in its cradle and turned, seeing Misty standing behind him. "Don't ask."

"Sit on the couch, and I'll get you cleaned up," she said, ignoring the hardness in his voice.

He sat on the edge, his body stiff and unyielding. "Get it over with. I've got people to see."

"You'll have to take off your eye-patch," she said slowly.

He ripped it off and threw it across the room. She inhaled sharply at the solid white orb sitting where his eye should've been. It wasn't glass or any other material she'd ever seen. It looked unnatural, like painted metal.

"Just go home. I knew you couldn't take it." He sneered.

She poked him hard in the chest. "That's it! All I'm trying to do is help, and you make me feel like I'm torturing you. I was a little surprised, that's all. Now sit there, shut up, and let me work."

His eyes widened then he chuckled. "Yes, ma'am. Do what you have to, and I promise to behave."

"You're still not going to tell me what's going on, are you?" Misty dabbed at the cut.

"I can't. It's for your own protection." He paused, looking like he wanted to say something else, but stopped. "The less you know, the better off you'll be."

She watched the peroxide bubble. "One day I want the whole story," she said smearing on a light coating of antibiotic ointment.

He caught her hands. "The day you find everything out, I won't be around to explain."

The tube fell from her fingers as he held her hands. He pulled her closer, and she went willingly, dropping to her knees in front of him. She gazed in his eyes as he ran his hand up her arm, stopping at her neck. She leaned closer, and his hand moved down, brushing her breast. She jumped.

"Why did you come along now?" he whispered, his lips just inches from hers.

"What do you mean?" She laid her hands on his thighs, slowly moving them up to his waist.

"Nothing." He leaned closer, his eyes closing as he captured her mouth with his, sighing when she opened hers to allow him to take everything she had to give.

He lifted her up to straddle his lap, pulling her shirt from her pants. He ran his hands along her bare skin, placing a small kiss above the opening of her shirt, then his thumbs rubbed back and forth over her breasts, teasing her into excitement. He kissed the valley between her breasts as his hands covered them taking her breath away.

She ran her hands through his hair, wanting to hold his head right there. Her body burned for him, and she almost cried when he pulled away, setting her on her feet.

"I'm sorry," he mumbled, walking to the kitchen. "I shouldn't have done that."

Heat rose to her cheeks, and she looked down at the floor, not sure what she should say.

He turned. "The longer you're with me, the more danger you're in."

Misty frowned, wishing she understood him. "I'd better go," she said, grabbing her blazer. Digging a receipt out of her purse, she wrote her phone number on the back and laid it on the desk by the door. "If you want to talk, call me."

He drank some of the beer he'd opened. "Misty," he called. She stopped, her hand on the doorknob. He pulled her into his arms, kissing her hard, his tongue delving into her mouth. "Thank you."

The taste of the bitter brew lingered there, and she trembled as he held her. "You're welcome," she said, struggling to get her breath back. He slowly released her, and she headed to her car on rubbery legs.

Chapter Six

Misty went straight to Rena's room the minute she walked in the door. She flopped in her friend's large round wicker chair, crossing her legs under her as she stared out the window. She glanced at Rena, stretched out on her bed.

"It was so weird," Misty finally said. "I've never seen a person go through so many mood swings in that short a time in my life. He's so complicated." She waggled her fingers at her friend. "A mystery that begs to be solved," she added in a melodramatic tone.

Rena rolled her eyes. "By you, no doubt. He's dangerous. If ULTRA's after him, he's done something heinous." She sat up, swinging her legs over the side of the bed. "Start using your head and stop using your emotions. Do some investigating. I bet you find something."

Misty got up to pace. "Are you jealous? No, don't answer that. Besides, who's been helping you learn to control your powers? And do I have to list all the times I've gotten myself out of trouble?"

"And into trouble," Rena mumbled.

"That's not the point," Misty said quickly, dismissing the statement with a wave of her hand. "ULTRA was wrong about you. Your sister forced you into crime, and you've done a lot to make up for your past."

Rena squeezed her eyes shut then slowly opened them as she pushed herself to her feet. "They weren't wrong. They gave me a reduced sentence because I gave them information, and Kristin vouched for me. I did my time." She crossed the room and grabbed Misty's arm. "If he's this escaped agent, how do you know he didn't plan meeting you? You could be next on his hit list, and you're too blinded by him to even allow that possibility!"

Misty yanked her arm from Rena's hand. "I think you lived with your psycho sister too long. You're seeing plots where there aren't any. Grow up!"

She stormed out of the room, slamming the door behind her, but Rena's words stayed with her. Even though she didn't want to admit it, her friend made some valid points. There was definitely something off about Taylor Tremain.

****

Jack heard footsteps approach even before whoever it was knocked. He pulled his gun and stood at the side of the door. "Who is it?"

"It's Frank," came the muffled reply. "Open up. Amy found some information we thought you could use."

He breathed a sigh of relief, grateful for his friend's ability to find him no matter where he ended up. He threw the deadbolt but waited until he saw Frank's face before putting the gun away. "Come on in."

Frank ducked in, shutting the door and shooting the deadbolt home. He frowned, eyeing the long cut on Jack's face. "What the hell happened to you?"

"Cyber-X. He got a lucky strike on me." He headed

to the kitchen, Frank right on his heels.

"Who cleaned you up? I know you wouldn't go to a hospital and you aren't that neat, so give. Who's the professional?"

Jack wouldn't look at him as he reached in the refrigerator for two bottles. "Misty. Now do you have something for me or not?"

Frank clapped a hand over his eyes. "I don't believe what I just heard. Why'd you bring her here? What if he followed you?"

Jack sighed, too tired to even get angry. "Lay off. I've had a bad night and really, I don't need to be lectured. She offered to help, so what could I say? Thanks, but I can clean up my own blood? That'd be like you telling Amy no."

Frank threw his hands up. "Fine." He sat on the couch and waited while Jack settled himself in the chair across from him. "Amy found out the conspiracy you uncovered went deeper than we thought. Your information barely scratched the surface. There was an inner circle no one knew about, not even the agents we pinpointed."

"Fenmore knew. He's an ass kisser from way back. He'd have to have known. He's probably still part of it."

Frank nodded, taking a drink. "I'm betting the whole thing is still in operation."

"And with Fenmore getting tight with Commander Frailer, he'd be able to warn them if the clean ULTRA was getting close." Jack stared at Frank, not really seeing him as he thought about this news. "It's come down to all or nothing this time."

Frank breathed deep. "I know. Maybe you should

lay low for a while. ULTRA's got your face plastered all over the news. Add in Cyber-X, and you've got problems."

Jack gave his friend a slight smile. "When have I ever played it safe? This time, though, I think you're right. I don't know what I'll tell Misty. She heard part of my conversation with Amy, and I get the feeling she's not going to let it go. I'll call her tomorrow and tell her I'm going out of town." He ran his hands through his hair. "I wish people would leave me alone."

Frank walked to the door. "You'll be here all night?"

"I think it'd be a good idea to keep out of sight for the rest of tonight." He shook Frank's hand before looking out the peephole to make sure no one was there. "I'll probably sleep in tomorrow. I'll call you when I get to the warehouse. If Misty can't find me, maybe she'll believe I've left."

Frank turned the deadbolt and grinned at his friend. "Do you realize how much you talk about her? That's a bad sign. It usually means something permanent is looming in the future."

Jack rubbed his eyes, then pushed Frank out the door. "Go home. I don't need this tonight."

"Good night." Frank walked down the hallway reciting an old childhood rhyme. "Jack and Misty sitting in a tree, k-i-s-s-i-n-g..."

Jack shook his head and closed the door. "I'll kill you tomorrow."

He collapsed on the couch, rolling his shoulders to relieve the tension. Misty was different from women he'd met in the past and yet, so like Carol. His wife hadn't put up with his temper either and had given him hell about it on more than one occasion. She'd probably tell him to go for it. He smiled. She would've liked Misty. She wouldn't have wanted him to mourn her for so long.

He liked the way Misty felt in his arms and the light perfume she wore. He even liked her clothes and found himself wondering what she'd look like without them. "It's got to be lust, pure and simple," he muttered, finishing off the beer. Admitting anything else would be suicide.

He banged the bottle on the coffee table. "I need a shower." He pushed himself to his feet. "Yeah, a shower."

He stripped off his clothes as he trudged down the hall. He stepped into the shower stall and turned on the hot water, letting it flow over him until it was too hot to endure. He slowly added cold water until it made the temperature hot but tolerable.

Bracing his hands against the wall, he lowered his head. He stood there, letting the water pummel him. He pictured Misty's delicate hands working the knots out of his neck and back. He could see her there, her hair plastered to her back as droplets slid down her cheeks, her throat, and her breasts.

Anger, hot and familiar, churned in his gut and he embraced it. He hated himself for wanting her and was angry at her for bringing back emotions and needs long buried. He snapped off the water, stepping out onto the small rug. Picking up the bottle of antiseptic she'd used to clean him up, he stared at it, remembering her light touch on his face, the way her skin felt beneath his hands.

Jack hurled it at the bathroom door, shattering the

brown, plastic bottle into a thousand fragments.

"Damn you, woman, get out of my mind!"

Liquid ran down the door in rivulets, dripping into an expanding puddle on the floor.

****

Jack woke at midmorning, taking a quick shower. He avoided looking at the shards on the floor as he finished getting ready, stepping over them as he went to the bedroom to get dressed.

In the kitchen, he grabbed a box of cereal and ate it dry. He sat on the couch, staring at the phone, before snatching it off the charger and dialing Misty's number.

"It's Taylor," he said. "Can I see you today?" He grimaced as soon as the words left his mouth. It wasn't that he didn't want to see her, it'd just be safer if he kept it to a phone call. *You blew that one, hero.*

Misty's voice trembled. "Of course. What time?"

"I can be there in about thirty minutes," he said, staring at the clock.

"I'll be ready. See you then."

He sat the phone back on the charger. She sounded eager, disappointing the small part of him hoping she'd be mad at him for his behavior the previous evening. He should stop seeing her because his day-to-day survival was so uncertain. He shook his head, knowing he wouldn't win this argument against himself. "Like telling Amy no," he murmured.

He called a cab, blinking as he stepped outside into the bright sunlight. After he picked up his car, he'd take her some place quiet where they could talk.

"Damn," he muttered. "This is getting way too complicated."

****

After hanging up the phone, Misty raced upstairs to change. She'd been thinking about him all morning, wondering if he'd ever call her again. "I just need to get to know him better," she murmured. Except for the mood swings, Taylor was really quite normal.

"So are most serial killers," Rena said behind her. "Your thoughts were way too obvious, even if I wasn't a telepath. He just called?"

Misty turned her back to her. "I'm not talking to you until you give him the benefit of the doubt. After all, ULTRA has been wrong before, why not now?"

"Fine."

"Good," Misty said smiling. "Then you'll see he's not what you think."

Rena frowned. "I hope you're right."

"He's coming to pick me up soon," she said. "Why don't you come down and meet him?"

"I think I will. I want to see your man of mystery up close."

She stabbed her finger at her. "And Rena, no mind scan, no telepathy, no powers at all. Understand?"

"Perfectly. Afraid of what I'll find?"

Misty just glared and walked out of the room.

"He'd better be worth all this aggravation," Rena grumbled as she followed her friend.

Chapter Seven

Jack studied the butler who answered the door. The man looked more like a bodyguard. He was short and squat, but the look in his eyes said it all. He was there to keep out the riff raff.

"I'm Taylor," he said. "I'm here to see Misty."

He hesitated before standing to the side and letting him in. "I've been informed you'd be arriving. I'll let Ms. Severin know you're here."

"Thanks."

He was led through the large foyer to the living room. It looked like this was where the inhabitants of the large house spent most of their time. Newspapers, a few soda cans, and other items were left in disarray around the room. There were several DVD cases laying on the coffee table, all popular romances. He smiled, realizing why there were tissue boxes at strategic locations around the room.

Jack walked around the room, trying to get a feel for the people who lived there. It looked like any ordinary family room. Pictures lined the mantel over a small fireplace and he studied them. Misty was in a couple with six other women, each of whom was beautiful in her own right. Someone behind him cleared their throat, and he turned, relieved to see Misty standing there with a breathtaking redhead.

"I'd like you to meet Rena. She was the one at the

restaurant the day you and I met. Rena, this is Taylor."
Misty stood back, watching both of them intently.

He couldn't help staring at Rena. She was
extraordinarily beautiful. He couldn't tell how old she
was, but then, who cared with all that thick red hair,
cascading down her back like a fiery waterfall or when
he looked in those midnight blue eyes. Her jeans and T-
shirt covered her completely, but he felt he could see
every line, every curve of that perfect body. He almost
missed the thin gold headband around her forehead.

His gaze drifted back to her face, and he realized
she was staring just as intently at him. His combat sense
began screaming at him. He felt like she was reading
every thought in his head, discovering every secret in
his heart. Right then, he decided to have Amy check her
out.

He shook the hand she extended. "I'm delighted to
meet you, Rena," he said, burying his suspicions deep
inside.

"Likewise." She grinned. "It's nice to finally meet
the man Misty keeps talking about. I was beginning to
think you were just a figment of her imagination." She
winked. "But I have to say, you are definitely real.
Well, I'd love to stay and chat, but duty calls. Any time
Misty can't keep a date, call me." She headed down the
long hall toward the back of the house.

Jack watched her retreating figure with interest.
The gentle sway of her hips held a lot promise for some
lucky man. He felt himself grinning like an idiot.

Misty nudged him. "Are you ready?"

"What?" He jerked his gaze to Misty. "Sure, I'm
ready. Does she get this reaction often? And why aren't
you jealous?"

Bedeviled Angel

"Yes, she gets this reaction from almost every man she meets. And I'm not jealous because I know her. She's not interested in you. You'd know it if she was."

She opened the door, and they stepped out on the porch. "Are we staying here or going someplace else?"

He escorted her to his car, opening the door for her. "Someplace else."

They quickly left the city behind as he drove far out into the country. Pulling over to the road's edge, he walked Misty up a slight hill to a beautiful tree with a large house towering in the distance.

"Should we be on their property?" Misty asked.

He shrugged. "They can't see us. We should be all right."

He couldn't tell her the house and grounds were his. Not after he'd told her he was broke.

When he'd escaped from ULTRA, he'd taken money from hoods, the mob, any criminal or villain he could to build the fortune he needed to support his investigation of the secret cabal within ULTRA and to help his team. When he'd accrued enough, he did some smart investing and, within a few years, was worth millions.

He'd wanted a house as far from the city as he could get. When this place hit the market, he'd snatched it up. The rural solitude reminded him of his grandparents' house in the English countryside he'd loved as a child.

And now, another summer was approaching and things hadn't changed since the other thirteen summers had come and gone. No reason to believe this one would be any different. He inhaled the country air, trying to settle his thoughts.

But something was already different. This year, he had Misty. He saw her watching him. Why couldn't she have been the fling he'd told Frank she'd be?

She leaned over and touched his arm. "So many expressions crossed your face just now. What're you thinking about?"

His hand curled into a fist. "I've got to go out of town. Not too long, just a few weeks." He leaned against the tree, closing his eyes. If he kept looking at her, he'd never keep himself together.

"We're not seeing each other anymore, are we?" she asked quietly.

His opened his eyes and gazed at her, watching tears slip down her face. "It'd be best if we didn't," he said in a low voice. "But I can't stop thinking about you." He laid his hand on her cheek, wiping away her tears with his thumb. "You're a dangerous distraction."

"Why?" she asked. "I can help you if you'll only tell me what's going on."

He pulled her a little closer. "You need to stay away from me, from what I'm involved in."

She grabbed his hand, holding it tight. "I don't want to stay away from you." He opened his mouth to argue, but she laid a finger on his lips. "I have skills you could use, connections with important people."

He kissed the finger on his lips, and his hand slid up her arm to curl around the back of her neck. He pulled her close until her face was inches from his. "I knew I should've kept this to a phone call," he murmured before closing the gap and kissing her hard.

"I can take care of myself," she whispered as he buried his face in her neck.

He raised his head and from the look in her eyes,

Bedeviled Angel

knew he must look pretty pathetic.

"What's happened to you?" she murmured. "Who's hurt you so much?"

He almost told her everything right then. Instead, he stood, giving her his hand. "I'd better take you home," he said, his voice rough with emotion.

Misty smiled as he pulled her to her feet. "Which home?"

"What do you mean?"

She wrapped her arms around his waist. "Did you or did you not promise to cook for me?"

"I suppose I did."

"I've decided now's as good a time as any," she said.

He smoothed her hair off her face. "I haven't gone shopping yet. I don't have anything to fix."

She mover her hands slowly up his chest. "Maybe it won't matter."

He frowned, picking up on her meaning. No mistaking. She wanted him. "Are you sure?" At her touch, his body came to life, responding to her hands quicker than he would've believed.

"Let's see what happens," she whispered.

****

Misty began to tremble as she stepped into Taylor's apartment. He pushed the door and it shut with a loud click, making her jump. His home was the same as before, increasing her nervousness as she looked around. The picture of Scavenger floated behind her eyes, making her stare at the man with her.

I'll tell him I'm not ready and ask him to take me home. She turned to tell him and stopped. He looked so alone as he gazed at her, her resolve melted and the

53

words died in her throat.

He took her hand. "Are you afraid of me?"

"No. Yes. I mean..."

"It's all right," he said as he laid his hands on her shoulders. He gave her a small smile. "You've been saving yourself, haven't you?"

She nodded, feeling her face grow hot.

He massaged her shoulders, helping her relax. "I'm as far from Mr. Right as you get, you know."

"I don't think so," she whispered.

"Say the word, and I'll take you home right now." He snorted. "If you knew the truth about me, you'd run for the hills."

Misty smiled as she laid her hands on his chest. "I don't know about that. I do know I want to be with you, right here, right now, whoever you are."

He ran his knuckles lightly down her cheek. "Are you sure?"

She nodded, closing her eyes.

He crushed her to his chest. "Then I'm a selfish bastard, because I want you, too."

He carried her to the bedroom, cradling her to his chest and set her on her feet. Slowly unbuttoning her shirt, he gazed into her eyes and ran a finger down the valley between her breasts.

"This is your last chance," he whispered. "Say the word, and I'll take you home."

Misty was silent as she finished pulling off her clothes. She turned to him. "I wouldn't stop you for anything."

She slid her hands under his T-shirt, caressing his skin. She lifted it as high as she could, and he pulled it off, flinging it to the corner of the room. Resting her hands on his hips, she slowly slid them around front to open the snap on his jeans.

She gazed in his eye as she removed the eye-patch. "Let me see all of you," she whispered.

He kicked off his boots, his socks staying inside and he pushed his pants down. She raked her gaze over his body, marveling at the strength in him. "You're as close to perfect as possible."

He shook his head. "No, I'm not."

She ran her hands down his sides. "Yes, you are." He started to say something, but she pulled his head down. "Don't argue with me."

He lowered his mouth to her breast, and she gasped from the shock that shot through her. Her hands gripped his head, and she pulled the rubber band from his hair, running her fingers through it to let it fall free. His hand moved down to her stomach, then lower, touching her gently between her legs. She grabbed his shoulders, digging her fingers in as he stroked her.

He laid her back on the bed, stretching out next to her and smiled as he touched her again. "I love the way your breasts rise and fall as you breathe." He trailed his fingers across her stomach before stroking the insides of her thighs. "How soft your skin feels."

He took her breast in his mouth again while his fingers squeezed her other nipple.

Misty's stomach began fluttering as his touch inflamed her. She spread her legs, inviting him to take her. "I need you," she panted. "Now."

He positioned himself over her. "Anything you want. You told me not to argue."

Taylor stroked the outside of her. He entered her slowly, pausing briefly until she ran her thumbs over his nipples, making him groan. He filled her, capturing her cries with his mouth as she moved with him. Her legs held him tightly, and they increased their rhythm, finally giving themselves to the passion exploding inside them.

He raised up and smiled at the woman who'd just given him something very precious, something special. She looked at him, a silly grin plastered to her face.

"What?" he asked.

"I'll have to tell Rena she was right, only minus the ripped clothing."

"Do I even want to know what you're talking about?" he asked.

She wiggled against him, smiling as desire again smoldered in his natural eye. "No. I don't think you do."

Chapter Eight

The phone jangled. Misty propped her head on her hand and watched as Taylor sat up and snatched the receiver off the cradle.

"Hello," he growled. She stared at him as he nodded his head, agreeing with whoever he was speaking to. He slammed the phone down and she jumped.

He shook his head. "Looks like dinner will have to wait." He grabbed his clothes. "We've got to go. Now."

Misty scooped her clothes off the floor, her fingers trembling as she pulled them on. "What's wrong?"

She frowned as he ignored her question, instead turning to inch the curtain away from the window. "Ready?" he asked, scanning the parking lot.

"Yeah." She stared at his profile. "You want to clue me in?"

He walked to the dresser, pulling out the gun she saw him with the other day. He tucked it into the back of his pants. "No."

Taylor led her to the front door and opened it a crack. "This isn't exactly how I wanted to end our time together."

She squeezed his hand. "I know."

They paused at the outside door and he glanced around the area. "We're clear."

She nodded. "Let's do it."

They ran to his car and she caught the keys he tossed to her before he slipped into the back seat and wedged himself onto the floor. "Head for the exit. If you're stopped, make something up. I wouldn't want to shoot anyone."

She nodded once, sure he meant what he said. "I've got it covered."

Misty glanced in the backseat. It was a good thing Chevy made their cars with a lot of legroom or he'd have never fit. *Thank God men never clean out their cars.* He'd thrown a blanket over himself and, with all the junk back there, he wasn't even noticeable. As she pulled out, ULTRA strike teams hustled into the parking lot.

An agent in familiar black and green armor waved her to a stop. She watched agents surround the building, packing an overabundance of firepower. She frowned. Did a couple of them have rocket launchers? Weren't they even thinking about the innocent people in the building? This didn't seem like the ULTRA she knew and worked with.

All this for one man? ULTRA really does have its knickers in a twist.

The agent leaned in, checking the interior of the car. "Did you see anyone leave this area within the past ten minutes?"

Her hands shook and she gripped the steering wheel a little tighter. "No, I'm sorry, I didn't. I work the night shift at my job and just got up. Did something happen?"

"We've been alerted to a wanted criminal in the area."

"Oh." *I shouldn't be this nervous*, she thought. *I'm*

an ULTRA liaison, for pity's sake. She noticed the agent taking in her mussed hair and rumpled clothing. She smiled as she realized the agent was looking down the shirt she hadn't completely buttoned up. "Is he hiding around here?"

The agent grinned at her. "Anything's possible. You'd best stay away for a few hours."

Misty gunned the engine. "Thanks for the warning and good luck." She pulled out of the parking lot, her speed increasing the farther she went. She was halfway to Angel Haven before she pulled over. "Okay, it's safe."

Taylor sat up, his hair and clothing as disheveled as hers. "That was quite a bit of storytelling. Have you always had this particular talent?"

She grinned. "Nope. It's a learned ability."

He slid into the driver's seat. "I'll take over."

Misty pushed herself over to the passenger's side. "Good. My hands are still shaking." She watched him for a minute. "How can you be so calm?"

"Practice," he murmured. "A whole lot of practice."

They arrived at the mansion. Taylor put the car in park and stared out the windshield.

"What will you do now that they've found you?" Misty asked.

"There're other places I can go," he said. "I've got to do some checking. I'll call you later."

Misty turned his face to hers and kissed him, pleased when he deepened it. She got out and stood on the porch, watching him drive away.

****

Jack pulled into the warehouse and sat there

listening to the ticking engine cool. He drummed his fingers on the steering wheel as he considered the possibilities. He figured he had three main options. One of his group had sold out, someone was captured, or Misty was somehow involved.

He hit the steering wheel. *"Damn it!"* He got out, slamming the car door.

ULTRA would leave a small patrol at the apartment, so that place wasn't good anymore. He stomped to the kitchen and grabbed a beer as he made himself something to eat. He could stay here and he always had the country house. He dropped on the couch and turned the television on.

He laid his head back, closing his eyes. "Bloody hell, I'm tired."

Footsteps crept near and he tensed, his combat sense kicking in as he stayed still. He counted to ten, then reached over his shoulder, flipping the intruder to the floor in front of him. He grinned. "Hey, Frank. I think this one puts me up at least a hundred to five." He extended his hand, pulling his friend to his feet.

Frank glared at him. "I hate it when you do that." He brushed himself off. "I came by to see if you made it out okay."

"I had help." He wouldn't meet Frank's stare. "Misty covered for me."

Frank cringed. "You did *not* just say that to me. Why would you take her back to the apartment?"

"None of your damn business," Jack muttered, feeling his face warming.

Frank stared at him and then burst out laughing. "Are you blushing? You are. Wait until Amy hears about this."

"Don't start with me."

Frank cleared his throat. "Could Cyber-X have put a tracer on you?"

Jack shook his head. "No. With all the sensors I have, I would've picked it up and he wouldn't have sent ULTRA. He'd come for me himself. He wants to complete his contract." He sat back down on the couch. "Has anyone been taken?"

"Not that I know of." Frank sat at the other end. "Do you think we've got a turncoat?"

Jack shrugged. "I don't know." He stopped, not wanting to voice his other suspicion. "It could've been Misty."

Frank just stared at him in silence. Then he said, "I'll bring the group here tomorrow night and we'll kick around some ideas."

****

The next evening, Jack pulled out the gear he wore as Scavenger. The green breastplate still fit him perfectly, but the blades on the black mesh on his arms weren't ULTRA issued. Those he'd taken from a villain. The gold gauntlets were another piece of stolen villain equipment. Everything else, the gray mesh leg armor, the reinforced boots, the leg holster, all came from his time at ULTRA. He checked his weapons. Everything was ready.

He still had a few hours before Frank and his team were due at the warehouse. If he could find out anything new, he would. He climbed in his van and pulled out. Time to get information, and there was only one man to see. He headed for one of the poorer sections of the city.

****

Jack leaned over the edge of the roof of a three-story building, looking for a particular man in the crowds below. Spying him, he jumped off the roof, his artificial legs absorbing the impact. He landed in the narrow alley between the buildings. He grabbed a dirty, disheveled man, dragging him into the shadowed space.

Jack smiled grimly. "Having a good night, Mexico?"

The Hispanic man shrugged. "Could be better. What up wit' you, man?"

"ULTRA's getting close. What do you know? And talk like a regular human being. You know I can't stand it when you talk like an illiterate slob. Save it for the cops."

Mexico straightened up, losing the heavy accent. "You're the boss." He glanced up and down the alley. "You've pissed off a lot of important people. Fenmore's goons got their hands on a telepathic tracker. You're lucky all they could get was a kid with no experience."

"Just bloody terrific," Jack mumbled. "Anything else?"

"Only that if Fenmore's involved, the kid's got to be scared to death." Mexico shrugged. "Other than that, nothing."

That explained how they found the apartment. A small bit of relief crept in as he realized this information let Misty off the hook. "Can you let me know if you hear anything new?"

"I need a new number," the informant said. He gave Jack a small, rumpled piece of paper and a pen.

He quickly scrawled a number and handed it back to him. "Try this one and be careful who you talk to.

Only a couple of us know what you're doing now."

"I'm always careful. I know who to talk to."

Jack pushed a wad of hundred dollar bills in his hand. "Keep yourself safe."

Mexico grabbed his hand and smiled. "You too, boss."

****

Jack walked into the warehouse, frowning when he saw the new television he'd recently purchased flicker. His artificial eye scanned the building, but he only saw a thin, dark-haired woman sleeping on the couch. He tapped her on the shoulder. "This isn't a hotel, my dear."

She jumped up, resettling her glasses. "Jack!" She threw her arms around him in a fierce hug. "I've been so worried about you."

He set her off to one side and began removing his armor. "I'm glad you're here, Amy. I worry every time you walk into ULTRA's bloody building."

She smiled, watching him lay the weapons in the footlocker. "Still treating me like the baby of the group?"

He patted her head. "You are the baby."

Amy chuckled. "You're never going to change, are you?"

"Nope." He pulled on a pair of sweat pants. "I guess you got Frank's message?'

"Yes. I came here when my shift was over. I went home first to make sure I wasn't followed." She shifted from foot to foot. "He said the apartment's been compromised."

Jack nodded, snapping the lock shut on the footlocker. "I'm not sure what else they know. I don't want you taking any unnecessary chances."

"ULTRA has no reason to suspect me. I'm just a clerk in the file room." She gave him an innocent smile, making her look years younger.

"You're not fooling me, my girl." She'd used that same smile many times in the past and sometimes on him. "You've got access to all those records and all that information. Just watch yourself."

"Yes, boss man," she said, adjusting her glasses.

Jack greeted each member of his team as they arrived. He looked at the clock. It was getting late and Frank still hadn't appeared. He'd finally decided to go look for him when his friend staggered in, his eyes red, lips pressed into a tight line. The rest of the team made room for him on the couch. Amy sat next to him and laid her hand on his shoulder.

"Jerry and Allen were taken," Frank said in a shaking voice. "I saw what they did to them. It was...I can't..." He stopped, taking a shuddering breath. "They're dead."

The team silently waited for him to continue. "They were definitely the rogue agents," Frank mumbled, looking at the floor. "How do they keep finding us?"

"They've got a telepathic tracker," Jack said quietly.

He went to the kitchen and poured himself a drink. Two more men, good men, gone. His eyes burned as he silently mourned his fallen friends. Gulping a second glass to steady himself, he went back to the team, handing Frank the bottle.

Amy looked up at him. "What are we going to do?"

"We get out of the city," Jack said. "We need to

scatter. They've got a better chance of finding us if we stay here. Head for the country house. Get clothes, money, whatever you need and leave. Amy, you're not going back to ULTRA."

"You need me there," she said. "I'm close to finding the evidence to clear you."

He waved her silent. "It doesn't matter now. The important thing is the safety of the team. Understood?"

Amy and the rest of the team nodded. "Yes, boss."

Frank paused before leaving. "You'd better call Misty if you plan to disappear. She may come looking for you."

"I'll take care of it. Now go. Get people safe."

There's so few of us left, Jack thought watching his team leave. *I don't know how we're going to finish it.*

He pulled out his repair kit from under the couch. A sharp pain twinged in his left shoulder and shot down to his wrist. "I should've stayed in prison," he mumbled, repairing the damaged area.

Chapter Nine

Misty walked slowly into the house, shaking her head. Taylor had been different ever since their second date when he'd gotten sliced open. His eyes held a wariness that hadn't been there when they'd first met.

Rena waited in the foyer. "Did you have a good time?"

Misty laid her purse on the small table. "You always know when I'm coming home, don't you?"

"It's my right as a telepath." She folded her arms. "So, what happened?"

Misty turned her back and slipped off her light blazer. "You don't want to just read my mind to find out?"

Rena shook her head. "That would be cheating. And I don't 'plug in' to my teammates indiscriminately. It's not right. I believe it was you who told me that when I first got here."

"This is true," Misty said, then grinned. "No ripped clothes."

Rena's eyes widened. "You were saving yourself for Mr. Right."

"He is my Mr. Right, thank you," Misty said defensively.

"Did you forget he might be dangerous?"

Misty turned away. "Don't start that again, Red. You need more than suspicions to convince me he's an escaped lunatic ULTRA locked away thirteen years ago."

Rena took a deep breath, slowly releasing it. "And they say redheads are stubborn. You promised you'd do some investigating. You're afraid you'll find something and have to turn him in, aren't you?"

Misty stared at her. "I couldn't turn him in," she finally said.

"You, madam, are a hero. It is your responsibility to apprehend criminals and hand them over to the proper authorities." She grabbed Misty by the shoulders. "Whether you like it or not, he may be a wanted man. You don't tell someone, you could be arrested as an accessory."

Misty pushed Rena's hands off and backed up several steps. "Stop talking like he's guilty. If I have to investigate, then so do you. You'll be with me, Red, every single step of the way. *Got it?*"

Rena watched Misty stomp up the stairs. "Oh, I get it. But if he hurts you, watch out."

****

At nine the next morning, Jack dialed Misty's number, shifting from foot to foot as he waited for someone to answer the phone.

"Angel Haven residence," said a female voice.

He ran a hand through his hair. "This is Taylor. I'd like to speak to Misty, please."

"One moment."

How do I keep this simple?

"You're up early," Misty said.

He closed his eyes, seeing her face. "I'm going out of town. I just wanted to let you know so you wouldn't worry. I should be back by the weekend."

"This has something to do with ULTRA, doesn't it?"

He stayed silent, not knowing how to answer her. "It's just for a few days," he finally said. "I'll be back before you know it."

"I want to see you."

His hand tightened around the phone. He wanted to see her too, but couldn't bring himself to say the words. "I don't think that's a good idea. I've got to leave soon."

"I don't care," she said. "Don't make me track you down."

Jack's resolve crumbled and he gave in to the urge to see her, hold her again. "Fine. Where do you want to meet?"

"Come get me and we'll decide from there." She paused. "And Taylor, don't stand me up."

"I'm on my way." He hung up the phone slowly. He'd caved in to see her so easily. "Pretty bad when you sabotage yourself, hero," he grumbled.

****

Misty saw Rena come into the hall. "Get that look off your face, Red."

"What look?" the telepath asked, her eyes wide with innocence. "I don't have a look."

Misty grabbed her purse, double-checking to make sure she had everything she needed. "Yeah, sure." She brushed by her to wait by the driveway, her friend right on her heels.

"Will you listen?" Rena insisted. "Since you're going to be with him, see what you can find out."

"Are you going to start that again?"

Rena grinned and folded her arms. "Yep. I'm still

not too sure about Mr. Wonderful." They turned, hearing Taylor's car pull in. "Speak of the devil."

Misty stuck her tongue out at her friend.

"I hope you don't act that way around," Rena paused, then said in a breathless voice, "him."

"One more word and I'll clock you!"

Rena fell silent, watching Taylor through the windshield. She narrowed her eyes at him before stalking back into the house.

"Did you two have a fight?" he asked as Misty climbed into the car.

"Not really. She's just a little too over-protective sometimes." Misty glanced at him. "Where do you want to go?"

He drummed his fingers on the steering wheel. "This was your idea. You tell me."

She sat back as he put the car in gear. "I have an apartment in the city. We can go there."

****

Misty unlocked the door and he stepped in, scanning her apartment, taking in the tasteful blue and gold furnishings, the small statues, and pictures of her parents and friends. He inhaled the scents of citrus and vanilla candles scattered about the room. A bouquet of early, bright summer blooms overflowing a clear crystal-cut vase sat on the light tan coffee table. Paintings of nature scenes decorated the ivory walls.

A flat screen TV stood on a stand across from the couch, facing the door, with a DVD player and small stereo system underneath. CD's and DVD's lay next to the player and stacked on the light blue carpet. A paperback with a bent cover lay on the coffee table by the vase. The room had a comfortable, homey feel.

He perched on the edge of her couch, his back straight, his body tense. "What did you want to see me for?"

Misty sighed. "I just wanted to be with you for a little bit before you left. Were you expecting something else?"

He narrowed his eyes, watching her every movement. "Why do you ask that?"

"This is starting to sound like an interrogation and I don't like it," she snapped.

"Then you shouldn't have asked to see me."

She sat next to him and ran her hand along his arm. "Why can't you just tell me why you're going?"

He stood and walked toward the door. "It's better if you don't know."

She came up behind him and wrapped her arms around his waist. "Then let me help you forget. Stay with me. Just for a little while."

He lifted her hand to his lips. "I don't deserve this," he whispered. "Or you."

"Yes, you do," she insisted. "You deserve so much more than life has given you."

His shoulders sagged and he hung his head. "If only you knew what I am, who I am."

She tugged him toward her bedroom. "I don't care who you are. Maybe later, but not now." She pulled a little harder. "Let me help you."

He went with her, holding her tight. He lifted his hand and pushed her shirt down her arms.

"I know I'm going to hurt you someday," he whispered.

Misty stroked his chest. "No, you won't. I don't know why you think you're such a horrible person, but

I know you're a good man."

He dropped his head to her neck, placing light kisses there and down her shoulder. He lowered her bra strap down her arm, sighing when her hands rested on his hips. "I'm not. I've forgotten how to be good."

Misty unsnapped his jeans. "I don't believe that, not for a minute." She slipped her hands over the bare skin of his hips.

He carried her to the bed and slowly finished undressing her. He smiled when she did the same to him. "You wanted me, my girl, so now you've got me."

"Can I keep you?" she whispered, gazing into his eyes.

"We'll see," he answered, pulling her close. "We'll see."

****

Misty jerked awake, the absolute stillness of her apartment invading her rest. They'd spent the entire day in her apartment, specifically, her bedroom. He'd glance at the door and then settle back in her arms. She could see he'd wanted to leave, but wanted to stay with her more.

She glanced at Taylor, the soft light bathing him in a golden glow as the sun started to set. He had a long scar down the middle of his chest and a lot of smaller, barely perceptible scars dotting his chest, arms, and shoulders.

From her hero experience, she knew bullet wounds and knife wounds when she saw them. As an ex-ULTRA agent, Jack McClennan was probably scarred like this, a small voice in her mind said.

No! she thought firmly. *Rena's wrong. They aren't the same person.*

She held him tightly, wanting to use his strength as a shield against the circumstances that seemed destined to tear them apart.

Chapter Ten

"No!"

Misty sat straight up, sweat beading on her forehead, her heart pounding. Sunlight streamed in, making her blink. She reached out for Taylor but she was alone, the covers on his side of the bed thrown back and the sheets were cold. She saw a small piece of paper, folded in half, laying on the pillow. Her hand shook as she reached out and flipped it open.

Misty,

> *I'm sorry I didn't say goodbye. Please understand I can't stay in one place too long, especially where emotions were high. I'll be out of town for a few days. I do care for you.*

> *Taylor*

She folded the note slowly as more questions rose in her mind. Did he just care or did he feel something deeper, like she was beginning to. And what did he mean about high emotions?

"Taylor, you're driving me crazy!" she shouted to the empty apartment.

She threw back the covers and picked up her cell phone to dial Rena. "Get dressed, Red."

Rena yawned loudly. "Good morning to you, too."

"Whatever," Misty said impatiently. "We're going to start your investigation today. I'll be there in about forty-five minutes. Be ready."

****

"We'll start in ULTRA's own files," Misty said when Rena jumped in her car.

"We need different outfits." Rena telekinetically changed their clothes into what they wore in their hero identities.

Green-clad agents hustled through the brightly lit lobby of ULTRA headquarters, as well as colorful costumed heroes. The two Angels nodded to those they knew as they stopped at the security gate.

"Place your right hand on the scanner, please," said the agent behind the desk. He handed them each a visitor's pass. "Welcome to ULTRA, Angels."

The file room was modern and well lit, but the musty scent of paper lingered in the air. Computer terminals hunched next to tape readers, microfilm machines, and rows of large filing cabinets. A large desk stood to the right of the door, a walk-in vault behind it. They approached the agent manning the desk.

"Good morning." Misty smiled. "My associate and I would like to see the files on Jack McClennan, please."

He tapped computer keys. "Do you have sufficient clearance? They're Class II security."

They pulled out their security cards, handing them over. "We're cleared to Class III," Rena said.

He got up and went to the vault. "Wait here." He came back a minute later, carrying a thick file and pushed a clipboard toward them. "You've got to sign for these."

Rena picked up the file. "Thanks." She smiled at the agent as Misty signed the sheet.

The agent leaned on the counter, staring at Rena.

"It's a shame Agent Rogers isn't here. She knows this case backwards and forwards. Actually, she knows almost every file down here."

"Really?" Rena said, getting a little closer to the agent. "Any chance we could talk to her?"

"She called out today. Something about her mom." The agent shrugged. "Amy's good about taking care of her."

Misty's gaze shot to the man. "Her name's Amy?"

He turned to her. "Yeah. Why?"

"I'd like to check with her on some other cases we're working on," Misty said quickly. "Come on, partner. Let's get started."

Misty moved to a back terminal as Rena smiled at the agent. "You've been a big help." She went to join her, waving over her shoulder at the agent.

Misty frowned. "And you've got to torment him, why?"

Rena shrugged. "Power glitch from the idiots at HelixCorp. I can't help it. It's programmed into me. I don't know what'll happen when I find someone I actually like."

Misty grinned. "The poor guy will probably explode."

****

A couple of hours later, Rena sat back from the computer screen, rubbing her eyes. "I got more out of the geek doctor on NewsLine than this file. It looks like a lot, but it's not. And there holes big enough to drive a Mack truck through. It's like someone edited out the important facts, leaving what everyone already knows."

Misty sighed, arching her back to get the knots out.

"The paper file isn't much better. All it says is Jack McClennan lived with his grandparents in England after his parents died, served a couple of years in the British army, and then signed with Interpol. His superiors were impressed with him and recommended him to ULTRA when it was just being put together."

Rena printed out the information she'd gotten from the computer. "He's certainly had a full life."

"That isn't all," Misty continued. "Here comes the 'wow' part. As paranormal crimes increased, Jack and his team were always there making the bust. He was just about the only normal human the supers were afraid of or respected, depending which side of the law they were on. He was promoted to field commander in just three years and had thirty agents under him."

"Definitely wow," Rena agreed.

Misty flipped to the middle of the file. "He went bad about six years into his career. It says he was selling weapons, secrets, anything he could to make a buck, to terrorists, paranormals, anybody with a lot of cash. His wife was going to turn him in, so he killed her. He appealed to Captain Starblast, but there's no record of what was said."

Rena took notes on the back of the printouts as Misty continued to read about his conviction, the trouble in prison, and the experimental cybernetic implants. She shook her head. "He's definitely been through a lot in his life."

They returned the file to the agent and Misty looked at Rena as they left. The telepath was too quiet on the way back to the car. Rena chewed her lip as she sat in the passenger seat.

"What?" Misty asked.

"Things just don't add up with this whole case." Rena turned to her, frowning. "How come there's no mention of what he did with the money or where they found it? ULTRA's hackers can find anything. And another thing. If he's such a high profile criminal, why are his records only Class II security?"

"You're right," Misty said quietly. "We need to talk to Captain Starblast."

Rena pulled out her cell phone and called the Challengers, making an appointment for the next morning to meet with the city's most popular hero. She turned to Misty. "Let's go home and compare notes."

Rena changed them back to their street clothes. She was silent for a few minutes, then said, "Misty, I'm afraid from here on out, things are going to get very complicated."

They arrived at the mansion and headed straight for Misty's room. The cheery yellow walls and flowered curtains were in direct contrast to their mood. The desk was neat with a few papers laying on top of a closed laptop. There weren't any pens or pencils in the holder so Misty grabbed a pencil and paper from her bedside table as Rena sat on the dark gold carpet with the printouts in front of her.

Misty sat on her bed, her left leg curled in front as her right dangled off the side. "Okay," Misty said. "Taylor lost his wife thirteen years ago. He grew up in England and was raised by his grandparents. His parents died when he was in his teens, he's broke and out of work, he's got a fake left eye and some bizarre connection to ULTRA." She looked up. "Your turn."

Rena tapped the pen against her forehead. "Jack McClennan grew up in England, lost his parents in his teens, was raised by his grandparents, and was in the army, Interpol, and ULTRA. He was accused of murdering his wife thirteen years ago. He did time, has cybernetic implants, including his left eye, and is currently on the run from ULTRA."

Rena looked up, staring at her friend. "Now, Ms. Severin, how much clearer do you need it spelled out? Taylor Tremain is Jack McClennan."

"Yeah, but..."

"But nothing!" Rena shouted. "Just admit it!"

Misty folded her arms and scowled. "I hate it when you're right."

****

The next morning, they stood at Challenger Headquarters, Misty's hand shaking as she placed it on the scanner. Captain Starblast himself met them at the door, wearing his light blue micro-chainmail, a white star emblazoned on his chest. His brown hair covered the top of his mask and curled at the base of his neck. He wasn't carrying the star-shaped shield he was famous for as he shook their hands.

He smiled as he escorted them down to the briefing room. "Misty, Rena, always a pleasure to see you. Your message yesterday was very cryptic. I hope I'm able to help you or answer any questions you have." They entered the briefing room and Cap gestured to the chairs around the table.

Misty sat facing the captain, folding her hands to stop them from trembling. "Can you tell us why Jack McClennan wanted to talk you after he was arrested?" She hesitated. "It's really important."

The captain stared at her. "I don't usually talk about that case. It was one of the hardest I'd ever worked on." He paused, weighing his words. "After Field Commander McClennan was charged, he called me. He'd insisted he'd been framed and others were involved. He had evidence and told me where to find it."

He pushed away from the table and began to pace. "I read it and he was the only one mentioned. When I showed it to him, he said what I had wasn't his original evidence. I checked his claims and found nothing to substantiate what he'd told me. I handed the evidence pack over to the authorities. There was nothing else I could do, no matter what my personal feelings had been."

He doesn't want to talk about this, Rena telepathically told Misty. *He's been through almost as much as Jack.*

Captain Starblast took a deep breath. "He accused me of tampering with his proof." He voice lowered and he looked away from the Angels. "That was the first time I've ever felt I failed someone who truly needed my help. So for the past thirteen years, I've been conducting a quiet investigation on my own. At first, no one would talk to me, but then I found signs he was right. And I believe it's still going on."

Misty jumped to her feet and leaned on the table. "You mean there actually *is* a secret group selling information under ULTRA's nose?"

The hero nodded. "I'm still gathering evidence, but I'm doing it slowly so no one suspects."

"There's a woman in the file room," Rena said. "Her name's Amy Rogers. She might know something that could help you."

"Thanks, Cap. You've been a big help," Misty

said. As they headed out, she turned to Rena. "We need to find Taylor or Jack or whatever he calls himself."

****

As soon as the Angels left, Captain Starblast made a decision to see Agent Rogers as soon as possible. He sat at the conference table, remembering everything that had happened.

He remembered walking into the weapons locker at ULTRA. He'd found the envelope and for a brief moment, he knew everything would be all right. Then he opened it and read the documents. The captain felt his heart sink all over again as he remembered reading the file that only mentioned his friend.

At the prison, he'd had to fight back the anger when he saw how beaten Jack had been. He'd wanted to go storming to the warden and demand Jack be better protected but knew in his gut that would've only made things worse. So he sat, silent and stoic as Jack read the file, then threw it at him.

He could still see the hate in Jack's eyes as he was led away after threatening to kill him next time they met. He felt his fingers curl into fists and he slammed it down on the table at the past injustice done to Jack McClennan. "I will set this right, Jack," he whispered. "I promise you."

Chapter Eleven

Jack arrived at his country house, entering through the back door, and heading straight for his room. He remembered the way Misty had looked as she slept, her hair fanned out over the pillow, the covers not reaching her shoulder, her breathing deep and even. Her hand had curled under her chin and she'd looked like an angel laying there. And he had snuck out. He shook his head, his heart aching at how he'd left her.

He threw his jacket on the bed and rang for his butler on his way to the bathroom. "Liar, thief, killer, and now you can add coward," he grumbled. "Keep racking up those good qualities, hero."

"You're home, sir. What can I do?" the butler asked outside the bathroom door.

"Is Frank DiNello here?" Jack shouted.

"Yes sir. He was getting concerned that you weren't back when you said. Shall I send him in?"

Jack ran water in the sink and grabbed his razor. "Would you, please?"

"Right away, sir."

"You summoned me, o master?" Frank said as Jack came out of the bathroom. "It never ceases to amaze me how you can change your appearance so completely. A wig and new eye color and you look completely different." Jack now had short, black hair and no accent. He'd put in contact lenses and presto, there stood one of the most successful businessmen on the east coast.

Jack threw a shirt and a pair of pants on the bed. "I was always good at disguise." He paused. "I have to send Amy back to ULTRA. I've got no choice."

"Why?"

"It's Misty's friend, Rena." He threw what he had been wearing on the floor by the hamper and dressed in tan khakis and a polo shirt. "Something about her screams 'hero.'"

Frank laced his fingers together and leaned forward. "How can you tell?"

Jack rubbed his chin. "If you met her, you'd know. When she looks at you, it's like she knows every thought in your head. In case she starts poking around, I want to know who I'm dealing with." He closed his eyes. "Amy has to go back."

"Isn't there any other way?" Frank asked quietly.

Jack shook his head. "Hacking in from outside will alert them." He laid a hand on Frank's shoulder. "I'm sorry."

The older man got up. "Me too."

****

Amy ran Rena's name and description through the database. Her skin broke out in goose bumps and her stomach turned sour as she read the screen that popped up. "Oh, brother," she mumbled. "This can't be good."

Her name was Rena Kalamus and she was a telepath, one of the stronger ones in the area. She was a member of the Angels hero team, her code name, Charm. Amy copied the entire Angels file, burned it to a CD, and stuffed it in her purse.

If Rena was a hero and Misty's friend, what did

that make Misty? Was her friend in danger from the two of them? Were the Angels adding themselves to the list of heroes trying to make a name for themselves by bringing in the notorious Scavenger?

"Jack, you owe me big for this," she muttered.

The desk agent poked his head in to ask her something and stopped. "You okay, Amy? You look kind of sick."

She gave him a weak smile. "Yeah. It's just been a long year today."

****

George Fenmore sat at his desk in the Council's hidden offices, turning a pencil over and over. ULTRA Commander Frailer was breathing down his neck for results. Not to mention, his own inner circle, the Council Leaders were not pleased by the amount of money Jack McClennan was costing them.

An agent burst into his office. "Scavenger has been sighted, sir."

Finally! "Assemble Alpha squad and my personal car. I intend to make sure there are no slip-ups."

"Yes, sir." The agent saluted and left.

Fenmore yanked open a bottom drawer on his desk and pulled out a silver device. He held it up to the light and studied it briefly. It was round with a flat side and recessed needle-like grips that would open when activated to hold to whatever it was placed on. He bounced it once in his hand.

"Now, Jackie boy, if this cybernetic scrambler doesn't make you see reason, nothing will." He grabbed his jacket and hurried to meet his troops.

****

After taking care of some business matters at the

country house, Jack retrieved his armor and went out as Scavenger to pick up more information. All of his usual sources were gone. He shook his head. Whoever said silence was golden was a fool. Even Mexico had disappeared and that worried him more than anything.

"Bloody hell," he muttered. "How can I do anything if I can't find anyone?" He hurried across the dimly lit, deserted parking lot, stopping short when Cyber-X stepped out from the shadow of the large, brick, building at the edge of the lot.

"We meet again, Scavenger," the mercenary said. He gestured to Jack's armor and weapons. "It's nice to see you're prepared this time."

Jack stepped back. "What, no shot in the back? That was pretty low, even for you."

Cyber-X shrugged. "Just trying to get your attention. Fine looking woman you were with that night. Anyone I know?"

Jack's anger began its slow burn in his gut. "I don't think so."

"Too bad." Cyber-X threw a straight punch at his target's chest.

Jack blocked it, catching him in the jaw with a right cross. The mercenary grabbed his right arm, twisting it up behind him. He pushed it higher and grinned.

"Just surrender," he hissed, "and make this easy on everyone."

"I can't. Not until I've finished what I've started."

Cyber-X shook his head. "All that time in prison, and you still haven't learned. What a pity."

"I'm no traitor, but believe what you want. It makes no difference to me."

Jack kicked backwards twice in quick succession, catching the mercenary in the crotch. He spun around, driving his fist down to keep Cyber-X off balance. Cyber-X surged up, his fist smashing into Jack's face, splitting his lip. Jack dropped, taking out the hunter's feet with a leg sweep.

Cyber-X yanked Jack to his feet and spun him around so his back was to him. Cyber-X wound up with a haymaker and slammed his fist with all the built up energy around it into his right kidney. Jack clutched his side as he dropped to his knees.

I should've upgraded this body armor. His breath hissed through clenched teeth as he watched the mercenary loom over him.

"Good work," said a nasal voice. Fenmore stepped out from the darkness, his squad lining up behind him. "Come to my office tomorrow, and you'll receive the other half of your fee." He scowled. "I should dock you for the time it took you to finish the assignment."

Jack glared at Cyber-X. "Damn you. You couldn't even work for the clean ULTRA. You had to soil your hands with him."

Cyber-X frowned. "What?"

Fenmore stalked over, pulling the scrambler from his pocket. "You may go, mercenary. I no longer need your services."

Cyber-X shrugged. "Suit yourself. I'll be at your office early and you'd better have all my cash."

****

Jack tried to rise to his feet as he scanned possible exits. The squad moved closer to him, raising their rifles higher.

"Don't get up, Jack," Fenmore said, a cold smile

on his face. "I like you on your knees at my feet." He gestured to the agents behind him. "This squad is my own creation. They've got firepower even the head of ULTRA doesn't know about. Try to run, and they'll cut you in half."

Jack didn't doubt Fenmore's words. The rifles they carried had only been prototypes when he was in. He stayed where he was, hoping he'd have a chance to get away and frowned when Fenmore waved a small device in front of his face.

"Know what this is?" Fenmore asked. "It's a cybernetic scrambler. It going to prevent your escape, and it's going to hurt." He grinned. "A lot. You don't know how long I've waited to do this."

He motioned two agents closer. "Hold him." The agents held his arms tightly as Fenmore pulled Jack's collar out and slammed the device against his neck.

Fire and ice shot through Jack's body and the needles dug into his neck. He screamed as he was let go and nausea fought with the agony that slammed through his body as he hit the ground. The slightest movement sent fresh, searing pain raging through him. His breath rattled in his chest as light exploded behind his eyes, and he welcomed the blackness that quickly crashed over him.

****

Cyber-X cringed when Jack screamed. He watched the renegade fall at Fenmore's feet.

He lifted his goggles, his eyes hard. He didn't know what Fenmore did to the renegade, but he did know he didn't like it. Yes, the ex-field commander was a criminal, yes, he was dangerous, and yes, he needed to be returned to prison. Somehow, he didn't

think prison was what Fenmore was planning for Jack
McClennan

He reached into an upper pocket on his vest and
pulled out a small grenade. He glanced at it, then
looked toward the agents loading Jack in a black van
and grinned. "Nothing says rescue like a good old
fashioned flash bang," he said, bouncing the grenade
once in his hand.

Chapter Twelve

Fenmore slammed his hands on the desk making the pens and pencils jump. "What do you mean, he got away?" He himself had brought the outlaw down. All they had to do was drive him in. "Can't you morons do anything right?"

"We got him in the van, when we heard something," the agent stammered. "We checked out the noise and got hit with a flash grenade. When we recovered, the prisoner was gone."

Fenmore glared at the agent. "So, obviously, you have no idea who it was or what they looked like, right?"

"We didn't see anyone, sir," the agent insisted. "Just the grenade. It could've been Cyber-X. He's rarely seen before he attacks."

"Cyber-X is on *our* payroll. He got the contract from *us*." Fenmore rubbed his chin, his eyes narrowing. "McClennan may have a larger force than we thought." He shook his head. "It's a shame those two agents of his didn't live through our questioning. I know I could've gotten what I wanted from them."

The agent stood silent, waiting for his next instruction.

Fenmore sat down at his desk. "It's time I had help with our tracker." He picked up the phone. "Get Donald Harrington on the phone." He glared at the trembling agent in front of his desk. "Get out."

****

Amy's grip tightened on her cell phone. "What do you mean he can't be found? You always know where he is, Frank."

"Not this time." He paused. "I'm worried."

Amy could hear it in his voice. Frank wasn't worried. He was scared, and she shook, his fear bleeding into her. "Call me if you hear anything, even if it's just a rumor."

"Will do."

Amy snapped her phone shut and stared at the stack of papers on her desk. She pulled a file from the top and opened it. The words blurred before her eyes as she read it three times and still didn't know what it said. I should've gone home, she thought.

An all too familiar and extremely unwelcome voice drifted to her from the outer office. *Not him. Not now.* She rose on trembling legs and went to greet the visitor.

"Hello, Captain Starblast. Can I help you?" she asked, praying her voice wouldn't shake.

"Good morning, Agent Rogers," the captain said. "May I speak with you privately?"

She smiled. "Of course." She turned to the counter agent. "I don't wish to be disturbed. This way."

Amy shut the door to her office, and the captain's presence dominated the small, windowless room. She leaned against the door, watching him sit in one of the chairs in front of her desk. She took a deep breath and sat down. "What can I help you with?"

Captain Starblast looked at her for a few seconds. "I want to speak with you about Jack McClennan."

Tremors raced up her spine, and she moved her

hands to her lap, wiping her palms on her pants. "Oh?"

He leaned forward. "I've recently gotten information linking you to him. I don't want to arrest him," he said quickly. "I just want to talk."

Amy sat back in her chair, silently grateful for any distance she could put between them. Her hands balled in her lap as anger fought with panic for room in her heart. "Now you're interested in him? When he was arrested, he came to you for help, and all you did was kill any chance he had of clearing himself."

She bit back the rest of what she wanted to say. If that outburst didn't tell him everything he wanted to know, she didn't know what would. If she'd had her gun handy, she'd shoot the bastard.

The captain closed his eyes for a moment. "I did what I felt was right at the time. I was wrong and that was an unforgivable error on my part. Is there anything you can tell me?"

"I've heard he's in hiding. Beyond that, I don't know anything."

Captain Starblast stood and handed her a business card. "If you should remember anything at all that can help me, or better yet, help Jack, call the hot line number."

Amy slowly rose to her feet. If she didn't know better, she'd swear her words had hurt him. "I'll do what I can to help you, Captain. I just don't know what to say."

He walked to the door and turned. "When you see him, tell him I'm on his side and always have been." He gave her a small smile. "I'm still his friend, whether he thinks so or not."

After he left, Amy laid her head on the desk. She

took a deep breath, trying to calm her racing heart. "When will this be over?" she muttered.

****

Jack opened his eyes and saw Cyber-X sitting next to him. Instinctively, he reached for his gun, groaning when the movement hurt. Soft sheets pressed into his skin. *Where's my armor?*

"That'll teach you to jump to conclusions."

"I feel like hell." Jack rolled his head back and forth, trying to ease the stiffness in his neck. "Where am I?"

"You're in my HQ, otherwise known as my house. You've been out for a couple of days. What'd they do to you?"

He took a deep breath. "Cybernetic scrambler. Every circuit in my body feels fried." He slowly lifted his right hand to his neck and found the device gone. "Where is it?"

Cyber-X grinned. "It's in pieces on my work bench. I wasn't sure if taking it off would kill you or not, so I decided to risk it. Seems you'll live."

Jack groaned again. "Don't be too sure." He tried lifting his left arm. "I can't move."

"I shut down your systems. I'll reconnect you now that you're back in the land of the living."

Jack sighed. "I think I'll pretend I'm dead. It's got to feel better than this." He closed his eyes, surprised his eyelids didn't hurt.

****

He'd been in bed a week and couldn't stand it anymore. Jack threw off the covers, standing on shaky legs. Cyber-X came in, shaking his head as he watched his "patient" try to cross the room.

"Get back in that bed," the mercenary ordered.

Jack took a few more staggering steps. "I can't. Just give me my gear, and I'll get out of your hair."

"And watch you collapse on my floor?" Cyber-X shook his head. "You've had all your internals rearranged."

Jack tried to call on his anger for strength, but his body refused to listen to him. "Damn it, give me my gear." His people needed to hear from him.

Cyber-X strode across the room, putting Jack's arm over his shoulders. "You can barely stand. You're in no shape to leave, yet."

"You don't understand," Jack said, breathing heavily. He pressed his hand over his eyes as his vision swam.

Jack sagged against Cyber-X as his legs gave out. The mercenary dragged him to the bed and got him settled. "Now stay put!"

"Like I've got a choice?" he whispered. He listened to Cyber-X stomp to the other room. *When did I get this ability to make people shout?*

****

Jack tossed and turned in the grip of yet another nightmare. He was falling...and hit the floor in a tangle of sheets and blankets. His eyes began their familiar ache and his throat tightened. He shook his head as memories of his wife, bleeding and dying as he held her, ripped through him.

Cyber-X padded into the room and saw him sitting on the floor, holding his head in his hands. "You all right?"

"Bad dreams." Jack looked up at him. "What time is it?"

"Around two in the morning." Cyber-X stood in front of him. "It's been another week. Feeling any better?"

Jack levered himself onto the bed. "Some. I'm sore and bone tired. I'm going to ask one more time. Where's my gear?"

The mercenary shook his head. "I still don't think you'll get very far."

Jack pushed himself upright and braced his hand against the wall until his head stopped swimming. "It doesn't matter. Look, you did me a favor. Let me do you one and leave."

Cyber-X just stared at him. "Why? I've been told, time and time again, you're a cold, ruthless, killing machine, but the more we fight, the more I'm having trouble believing it. You've had plenty of opportunities to kill me and my partner, but you always found another way. Again, why?"

"ULTRA has a telepath tracking me," he said, ignoring the question. "If they trace me here and find you're helping me, it's going to get ugly."

Cyber-X started to reply, then hesitated. He stared at Jack for a few seconds and finally nodded. "I'll get your gear."

Jack stared out the window, the nightmare dwelling on his brain. In it, Misty had betrayed him to ULTRA. Would she do it for real? He laid his head against the glass, grateful for its coolness, wishing answers would come to him.

Cyber-X laid his armor and weapons on the bed. Jack suited up, closing his eyes as dizziness overwhelmed him, again. All he wanted was to lay down, but he needed to check in with his team. He checked his guns and glanced at the mercenary.

Jack walked to the door and turned. "Thanks for the help." He gave the mercenary a slight nod, knowing he wouldn't be followed.

He stumbled to the street and signaled his van's tracking device. Sweat poured down his back and beaded on his forehead. His breath came out in ragged gasps. "Just hang on a little longer," he muttered. The van soon pulled up, and he climbed in and programmed the warehouse as his destination. "You'll be home soon enough."

He dozed off and on for the whole trip and soon, the van pulled in and parked next to his Chevy as the bay door closed with a soft hiss. He staggered out, stripping off weapons and armor, and headed for the living area. The last piece hit the floor with a clang and he fell on the couch, wondering how he'd made it home at all.

Chapter Thirteen

Fenmore sat at his private table in his favorite Greek restaurant. His stomach growled as he smelled yet another dinner, and his mouth watered from the spicy aroma wafting toward him. He'd already been there for thirty minutes, and still no Donald. He frowned. Donald Harrington hadn't been on time in all the years they'd worked together.

A hand clapped him on the shoulder as Harrington sat down. "Sorry I'm late George. I got delayed."

I wonder who she was this time. George supposed women would find him attractive. The sandy-haired man was several years younger than him, with bright blue eyes and sharp features. He mentally shrugged. None of that was really his business. "No matter. You're here now."

Harrington picked up the menu. "What's the problem? You said it was urgent."

Fenmore folded his hands on the table. "I'm having trouble getting my hands on Scavenger. The Council is getting impatient for results." He reached for the delicate goblet in front of him, the white wine sparkling in the low light. "Even the ULTRA commander is getting antsy with waiting."

Harrington laid the menu off to the side. "The Leaders said you had Scavenger and lost him. Any luck finding out who took him?"

"No." Fenmore scowled. "Those fools under my command can't do one thing right, and I don't have time to hold their hands on every operation. I've incorporated a telepathic tracker from HelixCorp. She's with ULTRA right now for training. The girl is young but has demonstrated an incredible amount of power. We think she uses empathy when she mind scans."

Harrington drummed his fingers on the table. "Has she tracked him, yet?"

"Yes," Fenmore said. "She led us to an apartment complex a couple of weeks ago. One of our agents said he stopped a young woman leaving the area, and he let her go without a vehicle search or even getting her name."

Fenmore shook his head. That agent had been dealt with severely. "This is the kind of incompetence I've been dealing with." He paused, getting himself under control. "The telepath, Mindspell, scanned the apartment and found psychic residue indicating the woman had been there with him."

Harrington rubbed his chin. "It would appear Jack has an accomplice."

Fenmore tossed back the rest of his wine. "And I need help with Mindspell. I know she hasn't had any field experience, but she always seems to just miss him."

"I see. So he might have two accomplices then." Harrington smiled unpleasantly. "I'll take care of your telepath. At least she's where we can keep an eye on her."

Fenmore knew all about how Donald took care of his agents. "Don't mark her. That idiot in charge of ULTRA doesn't know I've taken her into the field."

Harrington nodded. "Don't worry, George. She'll be fine."

****

Jack grimaced as a whistle screamed through his already pounding skull. He was in his bed with a glass of water and a bottle of aspirin on the nightstand beside him. Shaking four tablets into his hand, he drained the whole thing. The whistling stopped, and he tensed as footsteps approached.

"You look like hell," Frank said, placing a mug in his hands.

"Nice to see you too." He scowled. "Just because I'm from England doesn't mean I like tea."

Frank grinned. "Stop with the face, already. There's some of your best whiskey in it. It'll help you relax."

Jack eyed the cup and took a small swallow. He sighed, drinking more as tension left his muscles.

Frank dragged a chair over to the bedside. "You going to clue me in on where you've been the past two weeks?"

Jack stared at the cup in his hands. "Fenmore caught me. Remember those prototype rifles? They're not prototypes anymore and his troops are armed with them. They've got augmented armor, too."

Frank sat back. "You're kidding, right?"

"I wish I was," Jack said, shaking his head. "He hit me with a cybernetic scrambler. I was out before I hit the ground." He looked up at his friend. "I don't know how he did it, but Cyber-X freed me. I've been with him. He took that thing off me and helped me get back on my feet enough to get home."

Frank rubbed his chin. "Why would the mercenary

97

who's hunting you want to rescue you?"

Jack could only shrug. That was a question he'd like the answer to, also.

"Close one that time." Frank laid his hand on Jack's shoulder. "Get some rest. I'll be here."

****

Frank sat back in the chair by the bed and watched Jack slide down to settle himself in a more comfortable sleeping position, his eyes drifting closed as he nodded off.

Shadows grew long and darkness settled into the far corners of the warehouse as the sun slid behind tall buildings in the neighborhood. Frank turned on the bathroom light and closed the door until just a sliver spilled into the bedroom. He wandered to the living room, turning on the table lamps as he headed for the kitchen.

He fished his cell phone out of his pants pocket. Flipping it open, he hit the speed dial for Amy. She'd been beside herself with worry. How could things go to hell so quickly for them? He shook his head. It had all started with that damn NewsLine broadcast. He gave her a quick update, speaking in hushed tones so he wouldn't wake Jack. He flipped the phone shut and stared at Jack's desk and the CD laying on top.

Frank viewed the CD Amy had burned at ULTRA and knew Jack's suspicions had been right about Rena. But his friend had bigger problems than one lone telepathic tracker. Could he pretend ignorance about Rena and Misty until the truth came out?

Frank had caught sight of the heroes at one point and followed them, hoping they'd lead him to Jack. He'd tailed them to ULTRA, then to Challengers HQ.

Why would they want to hear what that back-stabber, Captain Starblast, had to say? But they'd never led him to the man he'd been searching for.

Frank had wanted to eliminate the two of them, to protect his friend and the rest of the team. He'd pushed his combat instincts aside, forcing himself to observe only. It wouldn't look good to have such a young and beautiful woman cut down and his friend would've been upset if Misty were harmed on his behalf. The grizzled agent thought about the computer disc. Then again, he might agree when he saw the data it contained.

Frank stared at the cabinets before opening them. He made a sandwich, thinking over the past two decades. The young Brit was brash and headstrong and Frank had taken to looking after him in his first year in ULTRA. Frank had been a veteran of paranormal skirmishes and showed the rookie the ropes. It wasn't too long after that Jack became his field commander.

Then Jack had been arrested, jailed, beaten, and finally escaping to live on the run for the past ten years. The renegade agent had gathered the team around him and supported them when they'd gone into hiding. Frank watched him organize, equip, and build a network that ran through the whole city.

"Fifteen years older than he is, and I'm like a naive schoolboy," Frank mumbled. "How can a man be so old and so young at the same time?"

****

"I need a vacation," Amy mumbled. Her hands had taken on a life of their own, constantly shaking. "I'm sick to death of heroes, villains, and this damn subterfuge." She slammed her purse into her desk

99

drawer. "I need a vacation."

When Captain Starblast sat in her office, she'd almost come clean, telling him everything they'd been through, after initially wanting to shoot him. Her supervisor had questioned her about the recent influx of people asking for her. If the clean ULTRA was getting suspicious, the corrupt circle wouldn't be far behind.

"Amy, there're some people here to see you," the desk agent called.

"Not again," she whispered. Sweat rolled down her back and, standing on shaky legs, she went to see who was at the front counter. She stopped, seeing Misty and Rena from the Angels team standing there.

"Can I help you?" she asked, surprised her voice didn't waver. *Great! More heroes.*

Misty smiled. "We're working on a few cases and this agent said you were the one to see because of how much you know about the files in here."

Amy held onto the door frame. She took a deep breath, letting it out slowly. For a minute, she thought they were here to talk about Jack. "Come into my office, and I'll see if I can help you.

Amy shut the door and gestured to the chairs in front of her desk. "Won't you please sit down?"

Amy watched as Misty looked around her office. She was used to the reaction. The small room was painted an ugly green, and it felt smaller than it was because of the filing cabinets lining the walls and her desk. There were closets bigger than this place.

When the Angels settled themselves, Misty leaned forward. "I need to ask you about someone you may or may not know."

Amy had almost relaxed, but Misty's statement

started her nerves jangling all over again. Her hands trembled, and she folded them on top of her desk, determined not to let them rattle her. "Who?"

"His name is Taylor Tremain," Misty said. "He has a scar down the left side of his face, wears an eye-patch, and has long red hair. When I was with him several weeks ago, I heard him talking about ULTRA to someone named Amy. Do you know him?"

"Has he done something illegal? Unless there's a file on him, I don't think I can help you."

Misty shook her head. "No. It's a personal matter. Nothing you say goes beyond the two of us."

Amy studied them. Any decision she made could be wrong and the end of everything they worked for, including their lives. The look on Misty's face made up her mind.

"I believe you," she said. "But I'm not sure I trust you yet, and I don't want to get into it here." She wrote on a small piece of paper and pushed it across the desk. "Meet me here at eight tonight. There are a lot of lives at stake, not just his. I'll tell you what I can, but no more."

"Good enough," Misty said. "We'll see you then." The Angels stood and walked to the door.

Amy stared at the door after they left. Frank wasn't going to like this, and when he told Jack, the sparks were going to fly. *What the hell was I thinking?*

She sat silently, feeling tears run down her face. "Let me have made the right call," she whispered.

****

Misty and Rena stood outside the small brick restaurant at seven forty five that evening. Summer had finally arrived in full force and they could feel the heat rolling off the building. Huge pots overflowed with colorful petunias and neon signs blinked from the windows. The door stood open, music and laughter drifting to them.

Rena glanced at Misty. "Is this it?"

"This is it," Misty said. "It's not exactly what I was expecting."

Rena turned to her. "After this meeting, things are going to change, aren't they?"

Misty worried when she heard none of Rena's usual humor. "Yeah and I have no idea what's going to happen. Thanks for being here with me."

"What are friends for?" Rena said, flashing a grin.

Chapter Fourteen

Amy reached the restaurant at five minutes to eight. She knew she'd tell Misty and Rena about the past if for no other reason than to have someone on the outside know their situation. Maybe, she thought, just maybe, she *can* help us.

As soon as Amy heard the description of "Taylor," she knew it was Jack. No wonder he was preoccupied lately. Misty was beautiful. She prayed again that she wasn't making a mistake. She squared her shoulders, took a deep breath, and stepped inside, wanting this meeting over with as soon as possible.

Her back stiffened as her mind received a telepathic message. *Over here.*

Amy scanned the restaurant, and when she saw a red-haired woman sitting with another woman with auburn hair, nod at her, she walked over. She laid her purse on the table, hesitating before sitting down. "I'm guessing you two are the Angels?" They nodded and she sat back. "I shouldn't be here," she said. "But now that I am, what do you want to know?"

Misty leaned forward. "Do you know Taylor Tremain?"

"No." Amy glanced at them. "I've never met that particular man."

"What do you mean?" Rena asked. "Is he actually Jack McClennan?"

The dreaded question had finally been asked. Amy narrowed her eyes. "Can I trust you?"

Misty nodded. "What I told you this afternoon was true. Nothing you say goes beyond the two of us."

Amy took a deep breath. "Yes. He's Jack McClennan." She shook her head. "I've broken the cardinal rule of the team. No outsiders. Jack's going to be upset."

"He's not going to hurt you, is he?" Misty couldn't stop the question.

Amy waved a waiter over and ordered drinks for them. She watched him go to the bar and come back, sitting their glasses down on small napkins. "Jack would never hurt any of his people. He'll just yell a lot and get all moody."

Rena snorted. "Oh, he's a typical male."

Amy grinned as she raised her glass in a toast to the statement. "Let me start from when I joined Jack's team. I was only seventeen, the youngest ever to be selected by ULTRA. Jack called me the baby of the group and Baby became my code name in the field. Five of us became the core of the Grave Diggers team. It was me, Jack, Frank, Phillip, and Carol."

"Who are the other three?" Misty interrupted.

Amy ran her hand down the side of her sweating glass. "Carol became his wife. The others you don't need to know about."

"How did they meet?" Rena asked.

Amy smiled. "It was at one of the Citadel's breakouts. Carol was attached to another squad when she saw him. He was standing on some rubble, shouting orders, shooting the bad guys. He looked like someone out of a swashbuckling movie. Carol got herself transferred and begged me to introduce her to him. The two of them immediately became obsessed with each other."

The waiter returned and refilled their glasses. Amy drummed her fingers on the table. When he left, she continued. "Not long after that, Jack became our field commander. Carol was his team leader and Frank was his squad leader." She looked down at her hands. "Carol was the only one to beat him in unarmed combat. He always said he let her win."

She sipped her drink. "The trouble started on one of our raids. George Fenmore was a rival field commander. He'd make like he and Jack were best friends and then cut him down behind his back. He challenged our team to take on one of the worst assignments ULTRA had. Jack thrived on the nasty work more than we did, so he accepted."

Amy stopped talking, squeezing her eyes shut. Minutes ticked by before she opened them, tossing back her drink. She banged the empty glass on the table, still not saying a word.

She took several deep breaths then continued, "We got to the location, neutralized the situation, and did the required clean up. We started going through the filing cabinets in one of the offices. Jack found evidence implicating a lot of important people in black market arms dealing, selling classified information, and things like that. He told us about it when our team was alone. He knew Fenmore was tight with a lot of the people on the list."

She stared at the Angels. "The next week, Jack and Carol were married. For the next two years, we worked on building our case. When we had enough, Jack was going to give it to the ULTRA commander."

Amy felt the now familiar trembling in her legs shake and her stomach soured. She squeezed her eyes shut as memories invaded her mind. This was the hard part. This was the part she didn't want to talk about, but had to. This was the beginning of the end of Jack's life. She held her glass until her knuckles turned white.

She stared at Misty, her eyes blurred with tears. "One night, Carol called me. It was close to midnight and Jack wasn't home. Frank and I went to look for him at ULTRA. Some of Fenmore's people were in interrogation. They tried to stop us, but we took them out. We knew they'd call Fenmore and tell him we'd been there. We found Jack in one of the rooms. He'd been worked over pretty good."

Her face grew hard, the words pulling themselves from her throat. "We drove him home, and he made us drop him off down the street. If something was wrong at his house, he didn't want anyone there to see us."

Rena held up her hand, stopping Amy. "Wait. Your thoughts are too strong," she said, her voice shaking. "I need to strengthen my shields." She closed her eyes for a moment. Staring at Amy, she nodded. "I'm okay. Go on."

Amy watched Rena's face, almost seeing every emotion in the telepath's eyes she herself had kept bottled up. "We saw Carol meet him at the door and drove off." She shook her head. "We were so sure they were okay," she mumbled. She wiped the tears from her face. "Thirteen years later, and it still hurts."

"What happened?" Misty asked.

"Jack said when he got home, Fenmore was waiting for him. Carol tried to push him away from the house, but the goon squad forced them inside. He refused to talk until they threatened Carol. He told them everything they wanted to know." Amy stopped, burying her face in her hands.

Amy felt Misty's arms go around her shoulder and she gripped the hero's arms tightly. She didn't realize talking about the past would hurt so much. She held Misty a moment longer before getting herself under control. She pulled back, smiling a little as Misty let her go.

Amy cleared her throat. "They didn't think he cooperated soon enough so they shot her. He didn't remember what happened after that, just Fenmore smiling that stupid grin of his."

"Hold on a minute," Misty said. "Captain Starblast told us when he got the evidence, Jack's name was the only one mentioned. How did they find it?"

"One of our teammates." Amy's back straightened and her fingers curled into a tight fist. "He was a new recruit, so when he was offered a bundle of cash to sell us out, he did. We discovered him and determined he wouldn't betray anyone else again."

Misty stared at her. "You killed him."

Amy nodded. "Phillip put a bullet in the same place Carol got it." She pointed to the middle of her forehead. "It solved the problem, but it wasn't very satisfying. Carol was still dead and the boss was still on trial for her murder and everything else."

She looked at them, narrowing her eyes. "Jack wouldn't let us testify on his behalf. He said he couldn't stand the thought of any more of his team getting killed. He claimed he let us down because he didn't go right to the ULTRA commander from the beginning." She shook her head. "We all knew the risks involved. He didn't make us do anything we weren't willing to do."

Misty sat back. "This explains a lot," she said quietly. She glanced up. "But where is he now?"

"I don't know. I haven't heard from him for about two weeks." Amy stood, grabbing her purse from the table. "I've got to go. I shouldn't have been here this long." She grabbed Misty's hand. "There's nothing more I can tell you. He's been made to look like public enemy number one, but believe me. We're not the bad guys."

She turned toward the door and froze. Fenmore walked in, staring at her, his usual amount of bodyguards around him. He nodded in Amy's direction, and the men with him watched her and the two heroes closely. She sat back down.

"That's the geek doctor from NewsLine," Rena said. "You're right. He does have a stupid grin."

Amy scowled in Fenmore's direction. "He's going to take me out when I leave. The big guy on his right has a silencer. You can tell by the way his coat bulges." She unzipped her purse, sliding her hand in. "Always go prepared," she muttered, her hand curling around her gun.

Rena reached across the table, laying her hand on Amy's arm. "Don't. Too many innocent people in here."

Amy looked at her. "You got a better idea?"

Rena grinned and winked at her. "You go with Misty. I'll distract them. Amy, give me your car keys. Misty, just go when you get outside. I'll contact you on the direction you went and meet you with Amy's car."

Amy handed her keys to Rena before letting Misty

hustle her out the door. "Is she kidding? They'll kill her without a second thought."

"Trust me. When Rena takes center stage, they'll never know what hit them." Misty glanced over her shoulder at her friend. "I almost feel sorry for them."

****

Rena watched Misty and Amy head for the door as she headed toward the agents at the table. The man with the silencer walked up to her and stopped dead in his tracks as he tried to pass her. His eyes glazed over, his hand dropped from under his jacket, and he stood there. Rena glanced as Fenmore and the other agent walked over to her. She lifted her hand just a little, stopping the other agent.

Fenmore glanced at his men and recognized the signs of physic ability from his years in the field. "I didn't expect to find a psionic here. Your telekinesis must be strong to stop them so completely."

"I'm in their minds, too. They're waiting for orders from me," Rena said in a quiet voice. "Back off, and I'll release them."

Fenmore took a step closer to her and frowned. "You don't know who you're dealing with, do you?"

"Maybe I do, and I just don't care." Using her power, she stopped him from reaching under his jacket and forced his hand to his side. "Don't even think of going for whatever firearm you think will hurt me. I'll twist that limb off before you even know what's happened."

"You don't act like a hero."

Rena glared at him. "And you aren't anywhere close to a paragon of justice."

"We just pulled out of the parking lot." Misty sent.

"Get out of there."

"Almost done with these idiots." Rena turned to the man in front of her. "You even think about following us, and I'll destroy you. We clear on that?"

"Crystal." Fenmore glanced at his men. "Are you going to release them?"

Rena turned and headed for the door. "When I'm sure we're clear of you. Stay away from us, and I mean *all* of us. If you're lucky, you'll never see me again." She frowned as she hurried to Amy's car. If Misty had known how serious the situation had been in the restaurant and how she actually handled it, Rena knew her friend would freak.

"We're heading north out of the city," Misty thought. *"You handled it in your usual way?"*

Rena mentally sighed. *"Of course. No harm, no foul."*

"Every time you say that, it sounds like you mean something else."

Rena was silent as the bright lights faded away as they drove north. *"No one followed us. We're good."*

They headed out of the city, pulling up in front of a large house in the country. Rena pulled up next to her and got out. Misty stood by her car and frowned as she tried to make out its lines in the darkness. "Impressive."

Amy got out. "It belongs to a friend of ours. He lets us use the place when we need to. He's in Texas this week on business."

Misty nodded, still staring at the house. She wrote her number on a piece of paper and gave it to her. "If you hear from him or need anything, call me."

"I will. Thanks again." She smiled as Rena dropped her keys into her hand, then walked to the double doors and disappeared inside.

Rena slid into the front seat of Misty's car and frowned. "What?"

"I've got the weirdest feeling I've been here before." She shook her head. "It's hard to tell in the dark." She pulled out, heading for Angel Haven.

****

Frank stood in the hallway, his arms folded as he waited for Amy to come in. She sighed, seeing the look on his face, knowing he was on the verge of losing his almost non-existent temper.

"Where have you been?" he asked tightly. "I've been worried sick about you."

She dropped her purse on the deacon bench by the door. "I told you. I met with two members from the Angels."

He stared at her, suspicion in his eyes, the look on his face, even the way he stood. "What did you tell them?"

Amy took a step toward him. "Are you interrogating me?" She stared at his face. "Fine. All I told them about was our days at ULTRA. They didn't seem interested about what Jack or the rest of the team was doing now. So, if you're done acting like a complete ass, I'm going to bed." She pushed passed him, heading for the stairs.

Frank rubbed his chin. "I gave Jack the disc. By tomorrow, he'll know everything."

"Then this discussion is over, isn't it?" She ran up the steps, turning when she got to the top. "I hate it when you pull this attitude with me, Frank, and it's going to stop. Got it?"

111

Chapter Fifteen

Jack stretched as sunlight pushed its way in through the dirty windows. He dragged himself from the bed and pulled on sweat pants before limping over to his exercise equipment.

He eased himself down onto the hard, leather seat and grabbed the hand grips. "This is the first time I've ever used this thing to get in shape."

After thirty minutes, his muscles trembled, and he dropped the weights, flinching at the loud clang when they hit the floor. "Feels like a bloody bus hit me," he muttered, pushing himself to his feet and heading toward the bathroom.

He sighed as the hot water worked wonders. He rolled his shoulders, not feeling as stiff as the day before. His stomach rumbled, and he snapped off the water. After toweling off, he threw his towel on the floor and pulled his sweat pants back on before heading to the kitchen. He slowed when he neared the phone and stopped. His hand hovered over it before he finally snatched it up and dialed. He wanted to call Misty, whether his instincts wanted him to or not.

"Hell," he swore quietly, almost hanging up as her line started ringing. He should just let matters lie, and let her think he ran out on her.

"Hello?" Misty said. "Hello?"

Finding his voice, he said, "Hey, beautiful,

remember me?"

"Taylor?" He could hear her surprise. "Where have you been? Are you all right?"

"I've been getting over a bad case of flu." He cringed as yet another lie came easily to him. "Did you miss me?"

"Terribly."

The warmth in her voice flowed through the phone line and into him. A tiny part of him leapt with joy because she missed him, and the rest of him howled in protest, wishing she'd hung up on him. He cleared his throat. "I'm still not one hundred percent, but I'd like to meet you for lunch."

"Sounds great."

Jack allowed himself a small smile. "I'll pick you up at noon."

Hanging up the phone, he walked to his desk and picked up the new computer disc laying on top of the pile of papers. Frank had said the information on it needed to be viewed as soon as possible. "You're trying to tell me it's bad news, right?" he murmured.

He flipped it onto the desk. There was always bad news, which meant it could wait. After what he'd just been through, what could be worse?

****

They sat in a rear booth of the dimly lit restaurant, and Taylor just gazed at her.

"You're not eating," Misty said, gesturing at his untouched plate.

His gaze never left her face. "And you've grown prettier since I last saw you."

Misty blushed as he held her hand. "Thanks." She looked up at him. "I didn't think you wanted to see me again. You left so abruptly, and then I couldn't find you anywhere."

He ran his thumb over her knuckles. "I'm sorry. I shouldn't have left you that way. I was trying to spare us both some pain, but I can't do it." He leaned across the table, kissing her lightly. "Care to tell me what you've done to me?"

She laid her hand on his cheek. "Probably the same thing you've done to me."

He stood, pulling her from her chair. "We'd better leave before we make a scene."

She nodded and they headed for the door, Taylor dropping a wad of bills on the table. He glanced at her. She was becoming important to him, scaring him more than he wanted to admit.

****

Taylor pushed her apartment door shut, sweeping her into his arms, kissing her long and hard. "Has it really been two short weeks since I last saw you?"

"It seems like so much longer," she replied.

He held her close, gently running his hands over her back. He lost himself in the scent that was only her. Everything was just as he remembered; the light, teasing perfume, the fruity scent in her hair, and now the musky aroma of arousal.

His nightmare slammed its way to the front of his mind, reminding him not everything was as simple as it seemed. He tried to force it back, but it hovered there, taunting him.

He ran his fingers down her arms. "I'd give anything to stay here with you," he murmured. *No happy endings. Not for me.*

She watched his face. "I don't understand."

He pulled her to him and held her tightly. "One day, you will."

He carried her down the hallway and kicked the bedroom door shut.

****

The late afternoon sun shone in through the window as Taylor cradled Misty in his arms. She draped a leg over his, sighing as she moved closer.

"I could stay like this forever," she murmured, holding him.

He closed his eyes. "Good things never last."

Misty sat up and frowned. "What do you mean? You're always saying things like that and never explain why." She laid her hand on his chest. "Tell me what's going on. Trust me."

He pulled her back down and held her close. "I can't."

She lay there quietly, remembering her conversation with Amy. "Tell me about your wife."

He said nothing for a moment. "Why?"

"I just feel that most of your pain goes back to her death." She stroked his chest. "You must've loved her very much."

"Yes, I did." She heard the grief in his voice, making it tremble as he spoke and it echoed through his body, his muscles tensing. "A lot of our friends said we were obsessed with each other." He gave a small laugh. "I guess we were."

Misty silently noted his words were the same as Amy's. Listening to him talk, she knew there was no way he could've murdered her in cold blood. There was too much pain in him, too much sadness.

"She must've been something," she said softly.

He nodded. "She was. She could play the roughest sport and beat everyone. Then we'd go to her sister's, and she'd care for the new baby. I thought she could do anything."

Misty rested her hand on his hip. "Did you have any children?"

"No. We hadn't been married very long, and we decided to wait. I wish, though...," he faltered.

"That you had someone who was still part of her," Misty said, finishing his unspoken phrase.

Misty had never seen so much misery in one person. When her parents were killed, it'd hurt more deeply than anything she'd ever been through. It didn't even come fractionally close to what the man in her arms had suffered. She'd had her friends to help her through the long days, the lonely nights. He'd had no one to share his pain with, no one to help him.

"Look at me," she said, turning his face to hers. "You've let the pain and grief build up for so long, it's beginning to destroy you. Let it go. I learned that when my parents were killed. You've got to grieve to ease the pain of your loss."

"I asked the so-called heroes for their help, and they turned their backs on me." Misty cringed as his voice turned hard and cold. "I guess I wasn't *good enough* for their time."

She shook her head. As an accused traitor and murderer, the paranormal teams would've done little. He must've seen that as the ultimate betrayal. She decided to tell him what she knew and to let him know about Captain Starblast's continuing investigation. Her own powers and hero status she'd keep to herself for now.

She closed her eyes, praying she was making the right choice. "We need to talk."

"About what?" he asked, his finger stroking her cheek.

"There are things, important things, I need to tell you. Things I think you should know." She threw back the covers and reached for her clothes.

He stayed where he was, watching her. "You're so beautiful, Misty."

She smiled and continued getting dressed. She brushed her hair back, catching it up in a ponytail as she watched him pull on his jeans, tucking the now familiar gun into the waistband. He crossed the room and stood in front of her.

She gazed at his face, wanting to see him as he was before bitterness and grief etched themselves into the lines around his eyes. She tried to see him as Amy described him, but decided that incarnation belonged to another place, another time. She wanted him the way he was; a man of no peace, no money, running from agents of ULTRA.

His right eye was so blue and clear, reflecting the inner turbulence of emotions roiling through him. The left, just the opposite, solid white, completely emotionless, the scar passing through it faded with time.

Dropping her gaze to his chest, she traced the scar there. He trembled slightly under her fingers, but remained silent and unmoving. She ran her hands through his hair, the softness of it in complete contrast to the hardness of his body and spirit.

"Are you finished?" he asked in a husky whisper.

"I don't want to lose you. Please, believe me..."

She stopped, wanting to say more, but not knowing how.

He put his arm around her shoulders, leading her to the living room. "Come on, sweetheart. We'll talk."

They sat on the couch, and Misty drew her legs up, trying to decide where to begin. These next few moments were crucial and saying the wrong thing would bring his guard up.

Taylor waited a few moments in the awkward silence, then said, "Where do we start?"

Gathering her courage, Misty said, "Tell me why ULTRA's after you."

He looked away. "I can't," he mumbled.

She laid her hand on his arm. "Would it make it easier if I told you I can help?"

"How?" he demanded. "You don't know the resources these people have, the amount of firepower they can get their hands on." His voice rose on every word. "They wouldn't think twice about killing you if it could help them get their hands on me."

She knelt in front of him, laying her hands on his knees. "I've found some things out, and I think, after hearing what I've got to say, you'll be able to tell me."

He leaned forward, folding his hands and resting his elbows on his thighs. "Go on."

"I met with..."

A knock on the door interrupted her. In the few seconds it took to get to her feet, the knocking had become an insistent pounding. "All right," she shouted, reaching for the knob.

The door crashed open, banging against the wall as it passed through her hand as she instinctively became intangible. She shot a glance at Taylor, but he wasn't looking at her. He'd dropped to one knee, his gun leveled at the door.

Cyber-X filled the doorway, his rifle held tightly as he stared at Taylor. "ULTRA's coming," was all he said and her blood ran cold.

Taylor stood, tucking his gun in the back of his jeans. "How soon?"

"Right now. You'll have to go out another way." He jerked his head toward the front door. "All the downstairs exits are covered."

Taylor strode back to the bedroom. "The tracker." He shook his head. "I'm getting too bloody careless," he muttered.

Misty trotted in behind, ignoring Cyber-X's heavy thumps bringing up the rear. She sat next to him as he pulled on his shirt and boots, laying her hand on his arm. "What are you going to do?" Her eyes widened in horror as he gestured at the window. "That's crazy! You're at least forty feet from the top of the building and a hell of a lot more than that from the ground. There's nothing out there!"

He grinned, winking at her. "Then I'm crazy."

Misty tightened her grip, trying to keep him from actually going out the window. "Don't do this," she begged. "I lo..."

He put a finger on her lips, stopping her words. "Don't say it. Save it for someone who truly deserves it and you." He dropped his hand and walked to the window. "This is twice I've put you in a confrontation with ULTRA. They're bound to get suspicious if you keep turning up where they track me." He kissed her lightly. "Goodbye, Misty. I don't think you'll be seeing me again."

Misty watched him push the window open and stick his head out.

Cyber-X came up behind him. "What's it look like?"

Taylor glanced over his shoulder at the mercenary. "It'll be a rough climb, but not impossible."

"Get going. I'll be right behind you."

Taylor grinned. "Hoping I'll reimburse your contract money?"

"Something like that." Cyber-X gave him a small push. "Now, move."

He pulled himself out the window, willing his body to blend with the building. Being seen would be messy. Falling would be worse. Scrabbling sounded behind him, the tell-tale sign of Cyber-X following.

Chapter Sixteen

Misty watched Taylor and Cyber-X climb the building until they pulled themselves over the edge of the rooftop. She slid the window shut as hot tears rolled down her cheeks.

"It can't end like this," she whispered. "Not like this." She pulled the curtains together and jumped as a furious pounding started on her front door.

Wiping her eyes, she stomped to the living room, her temper rising with every step. She was angry at ULTRA for always intruding, angry at Taylor for not owning up to who he was and trusting her, and angry at herself for not telling him immediately that she knew everything.

She threw open the door. "What?"

Three ULTRA agents in full battle gear flanked a man with short sandy hair in a business suit. A girl in her late teens with long, black hair, shifted from foot to foot and tried to stay far away from him.

The sandy-haired man whipped out a badge, handing it to Misty. "I'm Special Agent Donald Harrington. This agent," he said, gesturing toward the girl, making her shy away, "has tracked a wanted felon to this apartment. We need to search the premises."

Misty laughed. "Get a warrant."

Harrington turned to the girl. "Is she hiding him, Mindspell?"

"No," she said, her voice barely above a whisper. "He's gone."

"Where?" he barked, making her cringe.

"The roof."

The three agents ran for the elevator, Harrington right behind them.

Mindspell watched them go then turned to Misty, grabbing her hand in a tight grip. "I can't delay them, but don't worry. He's on the verge of escaping." She took two steps away. "I'm so sorry about all of this. I've tried to help Field Commander McClennan as much as I can, but they're getting suspicious. I don't know how much more I can do for him."

Misty shook as the despair in Mindspell's voice sent shivers up her spine. "What can I do?"

"Mindspell, get down here!" Harrington shouted, his voice ringing in the empty hallway.

"Tell him Harrington is still working with Fenmore. Don't forget!" Mindspell fled to the elevator.

Misty slowly closed the door. Mindspell had called him Field Commander McClennan. That put any doubt she had left to rest about his true identity. If only he knew how many people were on his side. Help was coming from so many unexpected sources. She sighed, wishing he were still here so he'd know he wasn't alone. None of his team was. She leaned her head against the door.

"Damn."

She picked up the phone and dialed Rena. "I need a lot of help," she muttered while the phone rang.

****

Jack sat for a moment to catch his breath after they made it over the top. "Bloody hell. I haven't felt this bad since yesterday," he mumbled.

Cyber-X eyed the roof door, holding his rifle ready. "You getting old, field commander?"

"If I was sure you were wrong, I'd beat the hell out of you." He looked up at him with a slight smile. "Right now, I just hurt too much."

Cyber-X reached down, hauling him to his feet. "If you want to live to recover, we've got to go."

"If I paid you every time you were right, you wouldn't be a mercenary anymore." He walked to the edge, eyeing the gap between the buildings. "We can make that easy. Can't be more than twenty feet max."

Cyber-X looked at him. "I can, but are your augmentations up to it? You've recently sustained a lot of damage."

Jack grimaced, not needing the reminder of what he'd been through. "They've got to be if I expect to save my sorry ass."

Cyber-X gave him a mock bow. "After you, fearless leader."

"I'm not fearless," Jack said, shaking his head. "And I don't lead anyone. Not anymore." He gauged the distance again. "See you next door." He ran toward the edge mentally cueing his cybernetics to greater power and leapt for the neighboring roof, making it with inches to spare.

When he landed, he heard something snap in his right leg. He cried out, dropping to the roof, clutching it. "Just great," he muttered. "Here I am in the midst of another miraculous escape and this happens." The only piece of him that never seemed to break was the artificial feedback circuit. Damn thing worked perfectly every time. "Bloody hell!"

Cyber-X followed seconds after, rolling to his feet near Jack. "What?"

"Something broke in my right leg." He shook his head. "And to think I just got done recovering. I don't think I can walk. Go ahead and take off. I can manage."

The cyborg hauled Jack to his feet. "Don't worry, I'll save you. Again." He pulled Jack's arm over his shoulder. "How'd you make it this far in life without me?"

Jack winked. "Just lucky I guess." They reached the door to the roof stairs just as the ULTRA men burst through on the other building. "I need to get back to my place, and I didn't bring my van. It has autopilot."

"I already said I'd help you, didn't I?"

Jack narrowed his eyes. "You will keep the location confidential, right?"

"I know how to keep my mouth shut." Cyber-X shook his head. "You really don't trust anyone, do you?"

"No," Jack said in a low voice. "I don't. I can't afford to."

****

Harrington narrowed his eyes as he watched the fugitives slip through the door on the other building. One he didn't recognize, but he knew that mop of red hair anywhere. So, Jack had escaped again, but just barely this time. Harrington blamed the slight figure at his side. He was sure the cringing little telepath was in sympathy with Jack, allowing the renegade to escape, time and time again.

He glared at the teen, then grabbed her arm and slapped her hard enough to snap her head back. He watched her crumple to the rooftop.

She rubbed her cheek. "I'm sorry. I'm trying, I really am, but I'm not used to this kind of work."

"Shut up!" he shouted. "It's your fault he keeps getting away. If I hadn't promised not to mark you, I'd shoot you right here, right now." He stepped closer to her, yanking her to her feet. "One more slip up and I might anyway. Do you understand?"

She nodded and winced as his grip tightened.

He shook her hard enough to rattle her teeth. "I said, do you understand?"

"Yes," she cried out, her eyes wide. "I understand."

Telepaths were an unpredictable lot, and he hated every time he had to work with one. As long as she feared him, he knew she wouldn't turn on him. He looked at the agents waiting for instructions. "You two take Mindspell back to ULTRA and secure her." He turned to the other agent. "Come with me."

Harrington marched toward Misty's apartment. She had to be the one Mindspell had picked up before. It was time to find out exactly how much she knew.

****

"Oh, Misty, I'm here," Rena called out as she walked in. "Where you hiding, girl?"

"The bedroom."

Rena walked to the bedroom and shook her head at the mess on Misty's bed. She'd pulled every bit of information they had and spread it around her. A writing tablet was balanced on her knee as she made notes.

"Are you investigating or do you need my help cleaning up?" Rena asked as she continued to look around.

Misty looked up and frowned. "Oh ha, ha. Like

you've never made a mess."

"Point taken." Rena pushed some papers back and sat on the edge of the bed. "So, why do you need my help?"

Misty stretched, knocking a pile a papers askew. "Now that we know that Taylor Tremain is really Jack McClennan, we can get on with helping him."

"Helping him," Rena repeated. She stared at Misty and shook her head. "Have you totally lost your mind? You know who he is. Call ULTRA."

"Technically, I did," Misty said slowly. She grinned when Rena just stared at her. "Well, we're both ULTRA liaisons, right? So, ULTRA has been notified, in a matter of speaking."

Rena threw her hands in the air. "You're nuts. Sure, he was framed first go round, but what about now? What about the other things he's done?"

Misty crawled across the bed, grabbing another article. "Are you going to help me with this or not?" She nodded when Rena rolled her eyes. "I knew you'd see it my way." A knock on the door interrupted her. "Again? Now what?"

Misty headed for the door as Rena grabbed her shoulder. *"Don't answer it",* she said telepathically. *"It's some guy named Donald Harrington and an ULTRA agent. They're here to see how you're connected to Jack."*

"You got a plan?"

Rena winked. *"Don't I always? Get scarce. I'll handle these guys."*

As Misty gathered up the evidence and used her power to fade into the background, Rena pulled off her T-shirt and grabbed one of Misty's tank tops. She shook her hair out and kicked off her shoes. She rolled the legs of her capris up a little higher and went to answer the insistent pounding on the door. Time for a little acting.

Rena opened the door, grinning at the looks on their faces. "Can I help you?" she asked, leaning against the door, her pose inviting them to look.

Harrington had flipped his badge open, then stopped, his gaze raking over her. Her low cut shirt was stretched tightly across her breasts, her pants low on her hips. "ULTRA Special Agent Donald Harrington. I'm looking for the woman who lives here. Is she in?"

"She had to step out for a few minutes. I clean her house a couple of times a week." She opened the door a little wider. "Do you want to come in?"

Harrington turned to the other agent. "Go back to ULTRA. I'll be along directly." He brushed Rena as he passed her. He sat on the couch, patting the cushion next to him. "I only have a few questions."

Rena sat close to him as she did a quick, undetectable scan of his mind. She felt his rage and hate and forced herself to keep smiling at him. "What do you want to know?"

He pulled a picture of Jack from an inside pocket. "Does she know this man?"

Rena stared at the picture. That's our boy, but he doesn't need to know that, she thought. "No. I'd remember him." She leaned closer to him. "You're not so bad yourself."

He reached out and pulled her into his arms. She slid deeper into his mind, stunned by abhorrent images she found there. She felt bile rise in the back of her throat while she read his mind. Every memory, every image in those memories was dark, with hate and rage competing for dominance for Jack McClennan.

She could see the things in his past that he'd done to be rid of the field commander—his co-operation with George Fenmore and another shadowy figure who exuded a lot of power with others in the background.

She was vaguely aware of him trying to paw her body and restrained herself from breaking his fingers and wiping his mind. You're a hero now, she reminded herself. You don't destroy people because they're mega ass-monkeys, no matter how much they deserve it.

She left him with a false memory of having a good time with the "maid" and retreated from his mind before she changed hers. When she was free from the scan, she practically pushed him out the door.

As soon as he was gone, Rena ran for the bathroom and threw up. She rinsed her mouth out and splashed water on her face then stared at herself in the mirror. "The glamorous life of a telepath," she mumbled.

"You okay, Red? You don't look so good."

She turned and saw Misty standing there. "When people are so corrupt, it makes me sick. His mind was like walking through nuclear waste, except worse. I just need a minute."

Rena went back to the couch as Misty grabbed two sodas from the refrigerator. "Thanks," she mumbled.

"So, what does Harrington know?" Misty asked.

"Everything." Rena stared at the bottle in her hands. She trembled a little as she recalled the hate that filled the renegade ULTRA agent. "Harrington and Fenmore work together and they both report to something called the Council. I think it's the same group that Captain Starblast is investigating. It 'feels' like it's buried deep inside ULTRA. This Council is behind everything that's happened to Jack and his team. They were the ones behind the black market deals, the information leaks, and Jack's wife's murder. They're the real bad guys in this whole mess.

"And now, the only thing this Council really wants is Jack McClennan stopped and killed. He thinks the telepathic tracker they have is helping Jack stay one step ahead of them. He wants to kill her, too."

"This clown seems a little trigger happy." Misty draped her arm around her friend's shoulders. "When you feel up to it, try to find Taylor. I mean Jack. I suppose I need to get used to his real name. He left here not too long ago, so he should still be close."

Rena gave her a weak smile. "I'll see if I can get him."

Rena expanded her mindscan as she searched in a widening radius for the outlaw. After thirty minutes, there was still no trace. She stopped and rubbed her temples. "It's amazing how completely he can disappear," she said. "Personally, I think he's just trying to aggravate me."

Misty smiled. "Now you sound like yourself. You think that about everyone you can't find telepathically. Rest for a bit. We'll try again when you're a little steadier."

Chapter Seventeen

Checking all of the scanners and finding them clear, Jack motioned Cyber-X inside. "We haven't been followed."

The mercenary helped him to the couch and eased him down. Jack reached under the sofa, pulling out his repair kit. He clenched his teeth as he carefully pushed off his boot and dropped it to the floor. "Ow! Bloody hell."

"That sounded painful. You want some help?"

Jack yanked off his other boot and slithered out of his jeans. "There's a bottle of scotch on the kitchen counter and a pair of crutches under the bed. I'll take both." Popping open his shin panel, he groaned at the damage greeting him. "You've got to be kidding me."

Three of his metal bones had snapped, tangling in the wires laying within. Jack sighed and began pulling out the damaged pieces, flinching every time a piece touched something it shouldn't. "Like playing a bloody children's game," he grumbled.

Cyber-X looked over Jack's shoulder, handing him the bottle of liquor. "I'm surprised you aren't howling with that mess staring at you. You don't do things by halves, do you?"

Jack took the bottle with shaking hands. "Do you mind?" He turned back to his leg. "This is going to take forever."

Cyber-X sat on the coffee table, swinging Jack's leg over his knee and taking the tools. "I don't mind in the least. You know, if you keep getting messed up like this, I'm going to have to start billing you for house calls." He lowered his goggles to survey the damage.

"I can do it myself," Jack said, his voice strained with the pain of the injury. "I have for years."

"Right. Shut up and let me work." Cyber-X used the fine nosed pliers to begin putting pieces back and moving wires into place.

"Where's your partner? She hasn't been with you the past couple of times we've met," Jack said.

Cyber-X worked for another minute before answering. "She's got her own assignment right now. One she really didn't want." He looked up when Jack didn't say anything. He grinned. "She's at a family reunion."

"Ah." Taking a healthy swallow from the bottle of scotch, Jack settled back on the couch, relieved to have someone else do the work for a change. "How did you find me? I don't exactly advertise where I'm going." He sucked air between his teeth as Cyber-X hit a sore spot. "Be careful. I feel all that."

"Sorry. I've been following you for some time now. When I saw ULTRA converging on the building, I had a feeling you were a little preoccupied. You should've been able to pick them up and get out on your own." He paused and stared at Jack. "You've got me confused. I'm told one thing, and you act in a completely different way." He returned to what he was doing.

Jack grinned. "Can't stand an unsolved puzzle, eh?"

Cyber-X glanced up with a smile of his own. "You don't know the half of it."

"Why all the help recently? I'm supposed to be your current contract."

The mercenary worked in silence for another few minutes before looking up. "I don't know. Maybe I'm getting soft in my old age. Maybe I just feel sorry for you. Maybe I'm a chump for wounded cyborgs. It could be, I got screwed out of the second half of my contract fee. It might be because I'm starting to believe you. It even could be that I just don't like *any* agency trying this hard to be rid of someone. Whatever my reasons are, my advice to you is don't look a gift horse in the mouth. You're not at ULTRA, and you're getting fixed for free. Mazel Tov."

Jack watched in silence as Cyber-X finished with the repairs to his leg, knowing he'd never have been able to fix it without passing out.

Cyber-X gathered his equipment and stood. "That does it. I'm done." He grinned as he slung his rifle over his shoulder. "Again." He took a step toward the door, stopping when Jack spoke.

"What's it like, having a partner?"

"What do you mean?"

Jack slowly placed the tools back in their case. "What's it like having someone with you? Someone you know will always be there? Does it make you softer than you should be?" He paused, staring at the floor. "It's been so long since I've been close to anyone."

"It feels pretty good, knowing someone's there. And if anything, it makes you stronger, more determined to win your battles." He laid his hand on Jack's shoulder. "Even if it does mean a tiny bit of vulnerability. Take it easy, renegade."

He listened to the mercenary's footsteps fade and, at that moment, was sick of being alone.

****

Jack woke from a short nap, stretched, and grabbed his crutches. He limped to the bedroom and carefully pulled on a pair of shorts. His leg still felt tender, and he could walk on it if he had to, but he wanted to make sure the repairs were holding.

He hobbled to his computer desk and eased himself down on the chair. He picked up the disk that Frank had said was so important. He sighed. Nothing to numb pain better than paperwork. He powered up the computer and froze as the warehouse door opened. His hand slid toward the gun that lay near the keyboard.

Amy walked in, heading straight for him. "Hey, Jack." She frowned. "Frank was right. You look like hell."

He relaxed, sitting back in the chair. "Thanks. You still okay at ULTRA?"

She shook her head. "I don't think so. The higher-ups are starting to get suspicious. There's been a lot of heroes in the file room recently and they've all asked to see me."

He took her hand and gave it a gentle squeeze. "Don't go back. Your time there is over." He smiled at her. She still looked like a teenager. "I don't want anything to happen to you."

Her shoulders sagged and she sat in the chair by the desk. "Thanks. I don't want to go back." She paused. "Phillip called the other day. He said you told him to be careful who he talked to, but he recognized me. He's got some information for you."

Jack flipped the disk in his hand. "What is it?"

Amy took a deep breath. "The telepath tracking you is female, roughly seventeen years old. Fenmore handed her over to Harrington and the girl keeps just missing you. She's trying to give you time to escape. "

She leaned forward. "I don't think Commander Frailer has any idea what they're doing to her. I think she's too afraid of them to tell him. Her code name is Mindspell, and she's on loan from HelixCorp." Amy looked at the disk in his hand. "That's the data Frank gave you?"

Jack tossed it on the desk. "Yeah. I was just going to view it. He told me it's information you found in ULTRA's files."

Amy stared at it. "So, you haven't looked at it yet?" she said slowly.

"No. I had to go out for a little bit earlier. I just got back a couple of hours ago," Jack said.

His mind was on Misty, and the way they'd spent the afternoon. He'd told her she'd never see him again, and he missed her already. Could he possibly be in love with her? He refused to consider the idea. She was a temporary distraction, nothing more.

Amy laid her hand on his. "Jack, don't look at the disk. It's not as important as I thought, and I need to talk to you first."

Jack stared at her, searching her face for why she sounded so nervous. First Misty and now Amy. His gut told him the two were related.

He narrowed his eyes, trying to see her thoughts. "Talk to me. What's up?"

Amy looked everywhere but at him. "I...met with some people who were asking questions about you."

Dread crawled up his spine. Had his friend been forced? Did they hurt her? "Who, Amy?" He watched tears slip down her cheeks. "Listen to me. Whatever happened, we'll get through it, all right? Just tell me."

She began crying. "I'm sorry, Jack. They said they only had personal interest in you."

"Who, Amy?" he said, his voice rising. Great. Now he was beginning to make himself shout. Pretty good ability when it works on you, too.

She wiped her eyes. "That girl you're seeing and her friend. Frank told me who she was, and I thought it would be okay. All she wanted to know about were our days at ULTRA. She didn't seem interested in what you were doing currently."

Jack stood and pulled Amy into his arms, letting her cry. Misty knew about him. That must've been what she wanted to talk about and why she'd asked about his wife. Relief surged through him. No more lies, not to Misty. He could reclaim, at least, a small part of himself.

As Amy cried into his shirt, guilt niggled at him. The fact that she thought he'd be angry with her was brought her to this point. She'd never been meant for subterfuge. Amy had always led the frontal attack and always, *always*, took the direct approach to everything she did. Yet, he'd given her the worst of all possible assignments—sneaking files out of ULTRA.

He held her tightly. "I'm sorry, Amy. You weren't meant for this, and I knew it. I was with her this afternoon. I told her I can't see her any more. Don't worry. You've done me no harm." He wiped her eyes with the bottom of his T-shirt. "No more tears?"

She smiled. "No more tears. You're really not mad

about me talking to her? Frank said you'd have a fit."

Jack kissed the top of her head. "I could no more be mad at you than Frank could. Go on home and don't worry. Everything's fine."

She cleaned her glasses with her shirt. "I'll call you when I get to the country house. I've got to stop by my apartment first and get a few things. I should be at the house by dinner time."

He nodded, glad she was leaving the city. "Sounds good. If Frank is there, tell him I'll call him later."

"I will. See you."

****

Jack pushed the disk into the waiting computer. "Might as well see what's got everyone so upset."

The file name came up and he frowned, leaning closer to the screen. It read simply, "Angels." He'd heard of them. An all-female band of heroes, their legal status still under hot debate amongst law enforcement agencies. Why would his people think this was important enough to show him? He knew about this team.

Pictures and information began popping up on the screen. He skipped over the first few pictures. He'd seen pictures of the Angels before and knew all their code names. A redhead wearing a gold headband stopped him. The name under the picture read Charm a.k.a. Rena Kalamus. This was Misty's friend who always looked like she didn't trust him. Rena, he continued reading, was one of the stronger telepaths in the city.

The last picture commanded his attention. Mist. Her paranormal ability is to pass out of the real world and into a desolid state, like a ghost. He enlarged the picture, using the computer to remove the white domino mask she wore, knowing who he'd find beneath. Misty, his beautiful Misty, stared back at him. She was one of them. One of the untrustworthy. A hero.

Jack paced the length of the warehouse several times, his crutches, his pain, forgotten. No wonder her home was called Angel Haven. It truly was a haven for the Angels, a safe place for the team to recover and regroup. Dismay fled, leaving only anger and betrayal in its wake. He had no more questions now about how ULTRA kept finding him. Her file listed her as an ULTRA liaison. She was tight with the people hunting him. What lies had she told Amy to get her to open up?

He stomped into the bedroom, banging open the footlocker to grab his gear and caught sight of his reflection in the breastplate, thinking he looked older than he should. "What's happened to me?" He lowered the armor, then, remembering what he learned, raised it again.

His anger clawed its way to the surface, this time directed at himself. He, the mighty, untouchable Scavenger, had finally been snared in one of ULTRA's traps. All it took was a pretty face.

He marched to the door. "Well, my girl, you won't catch me so easily."

****

Amy shut the door to her apartment and threw her keys on the table. The lights came on and she swung around, seeing four of Fenmore's squad there. She caught the man nearest her with a solid punch to his throat and kicked out at the other man behind her. She caught the arm of a third and twisted it behind him, pushing it up. The last agent clubbed her, making her drop her hold on the man before falling to her knees. She was grabbed and taken to Fenmore, who was lounging in her recliner.

"Good evening, Agent Rogers," he said, watching her closely.

Amy glared at him, her hands curled into fists. "What do you want?"

He stood. "Information. Take her to the interrogation site. I'll be along directly."

Amy struggled, making the guards work to drag her up the roof stairs. She knew people wouldn't be looking for her right away. She pressed her lips tightly together.

I won't let the team down. Even if I don't make it, they'll never learn anything from me.

Her only regret as the ULTRA shuttle took off was that Jack would never know how close their enemies were getting.

Chapter Eighteen

Jack's surveillance equipment told him Misty was still home. He frowned. How much did she know? And what should he do with her afterwards? That was the real question.

He dropped a thin cable over the side of the building, checked to make sure it was anchored and paused. What was he doing here? Misty had completely, in every way, given herself to him. Maybe there was a simple explanation for her involvement with ULTRA. Maybe she *was* trying to help him. He closed his eyes and hung his head.

"And now you question your own actions," he muttered. "You're a bloody mess, hero."

Misty was a special woman and, without question, had done what he'd asked. But that was the whole point, wasn't it? She'd been extremely calm in the face of severe emergencies. She hadn't panicked when Cyber-X burst into her apartment, but had been terrified for his safety when he climbed the building.

He shook his head. No. He was right. As an ULTRA liaison, she had an obligation to bring him in. He ignored the little voice that said he was as big a liar as Misty, because if he listened, that little voice would be his undoing.

He dropped silently to the bedroom floor, listening to her move around in the living room. He walked out, carrying his rifle.

"Hello, hero," he sneered.

Misty spun around, dropping the clippings she'd carried out from her bedroom. She started toward him, stopping when he raised the rifle a little higher.

"Taylor, I..."

He held up a hand, stopping her. "There is no Taylor Tremain. There's only ever been Jack McClennan. So you may as well get used to my real name. How long have you known who I am?"

She backed up as he moved toward her, only stopping when she hit the wall. "Only for a couple of weeks. I tried to tell you the last time you were here. You need to know how many people are on your side, trying to help you and your team."

Jack's slow burn of anger built to a furious rage as he stalked forward, stopping just inches from her. "So, you went digging into my past and interrogated my friend."

"I just want to help you," she whispered.

"Help me? I've heard that lie before. Can't you come up with something original?"

Jack watched her face as he kept her pinned to the wall. He could see the tears in her eyes, but whether it was because he was intentionally cruel, or because she'd been found out, he wasn't sure. He caught himself leaning down to kiss her and forced himself to walk away from her. *How can I still want her, even knowing what she is?*

He kept his back to her when he spoke again. "Were you planning on telling me about your own powers, or would that fact have been conveniently left out?"

He listened to her quiet footsteps as she came up behind him. "I wouldn't have told you. I thought it best to drop one surprise on you at a time. You'd just finished telling me how you felt about the hero community."

He whirled around to face her. "This all fits together a little too neatly. Who's your contact at ULTRA?"

"What?"

He grabbed her arm. "It seems odd that after I meet you, ULTRA starts showing up after leaving me alone for pretty much the past ten years. I suppose it's because you're on their payroll. Who are you supposed to call when we're together? Is someone coming now? Is the telepath in on it?"

She laid her hand on his chest. "I've never called ULTRA about you. I did call Rena, but she's helping me clear you. I was born with my powers so that shouldn't even be a factor. I care for you."

He narrowed his eyes, staring at her. "Even now? You can stand there and honestly say you care without knowing what I'll do next?"

"I can and I do. If you'd stop being such an idiot, you'd see that," she said, her defiance trying to force its way out.

He pulled her closer to him. "But you're afraid of me. Don't deny it. It's in your eyes, the way you're standing. I've seen it too many times to count." He let go of her, stepping back. "You should be afraid of me. I'm insane, you know. It's there, in all those records you poured over so faithfully."

"No, it isn't!"

"Yes, it is. You just have to know how to read it."

He tapped the side of his skull. "I should be locked away. I'm a danger to others and a menace to society. The old sanity could go at any time."

She grabbed his arms. "Stop it! It isn't true! They were lying so there was a reason to lock you away. Let me help you. Trust me!"

He laughed, watching her cringe at the harsh sound. "Trust you?" His voice was hard, cold. "I don't trust any hero. Ever!"

He grabbed her around the waist, carrying her with little effort to the bedroom window. "I want to show you something." He took them up the cable he'd left to the roof.

He dragged her to the edge of the roof and made her look over the side. "You see those people down there? They don't need you heroes or want you. Want to know why? It's because you ask for trust and give none in return."

He pulled her back, turning her to face him. "You want to help me? Don't. I don't need your help and I don't need you!"

He shoved her away from him, standing over her where she fell to the rooftop. "I expect you to stay out of my life, Misty. Don't make me warn you again."

He jumped to the next roof, disappearing into the blackness beyond.

****

When Jack had burst into her living room, Misty was overjoyed. Now she could tell him all she knew. Then she'd spied the armor, the weapons, and the anger simmering in him. The muscle in his cheek twitched like it had when he'd been sliced open the night of their second date. It was true that if looks could kill, she would've been six feet under. Maybe more.

She'd been trembling since she'd felt the fury radiate from him. He'd known she was afraid of him, and he'd been right. If only he'd listened to her, but he'd been betrayed by people and heroes he'd trusted in the past. She understood it would make him wary of any hero and it would take time to rebuild that trust. That still didn't make it hurt any less.

She turned intangible and passed through the roof and the hallways of the upper floors to fade into her apartment. She walked slowly to her bedroom, huddling miserably on the bed, holding a pillow to her chest. She kept hearing him say he didn't need her and those words would fuel another round of tears. She was like that when Rena returned.

****

Amy had been hanging by her wrists for almost an hour. Some agents would've cracked with waiting, not being able to stand the suspense. She'd been through this before, except this time, no team would be coming to her rescue.

She looked around. Definitely some type of abandoned warehouse, four agents, and one chair. One agent kept glancing at her, and she knew he was going to try something. She watched him saunter over.

He grabbed her chin. "Not very pretty, are you? I wonder if you'll last as long as the other two. All this loyalty for one man." He grinned at his partner. "I know why she's loyal." He moved closer to her. "Come on, sweetheart. Give us a little of what you're giving good old Jack."

He pulled her hair back, kissing her hard. When he started fumbling with her jeans, she clamped her teeth

143

down on his lip, at the same time bringing her knee up into his groin. He staggered back and she pulled herself up on the ropes that held her and kicked him in the chest.

"And I know why you can't get into the real ULTRA," she growled. "You're just not good enough."

The other agent backhanded her, knocking her glasses to the floor. "Keep your mouth shut!"

Fenmore arrived as the agent balled up a fist and drew his arm back. He waved the man away and pulled the chair over. He stared at Amy as he sat down, crossing his legs. "Now, Agent Rogers, tell me about Jack McClennan, and we can all go home."

Amy turned her most charming smile to him. "He's six foot five. He has red hair. He's a good man and better than you at everything, including breathing."

He scowled. "It seems Jack's defiance has rubbed off on you. You used to be so much more reasonable, but I had a feeling you'd be stubborn."

"I was reasonable before you decided to ruin Jack and our team. I was reasonable before I found out what you are."

Fenmore looked at the agents around him. "We're in for a long night."

Amy turned her head and closed her eyes. *If anyone's out there, please help me.*

With all the psionics in the city, hopefully someone would pick up her telepathic cry.

Chapter Nineteen

Rena came by to see if Misty had heard anything else from Jack, and found her in the bedroom, curled up on the bed, holding a pillow to her chest. She rubbed her friend's shoulder and held her hand while Misty told her everything that happened between her and Jack. The more she talked, the more Rena's temper simmered.

"It'll be okay. He was just surprised, that's all." She paused. "Is he really worth all this grief?"

Misty nodded. "That's the only thing I *am* sure of." Tears rolled down her cheeks again.

Rena sighed, wishing there was something she could say. "Things will work out. You'll see." She stood and went to the door. "You sure you don't want me to stay? I can put off doing stuff if you need me to."

"I'll be all right. Go run your errands. Call me when you get back to the mansion."

Rena left the apartment, stomping to the garage. Her sister would've been proud of how she'd held onto her temper. Of all the unmitigated gall of that man! Rena was sure if she saw him, she'd strangle him.

"That stupid, pompous, overbearing, complete, and total bastard!"

She climbed into her car, slamming the door so hard the loose bolt holding her rearview mirror creaked, and it tilted. She took several deep breaths, adjusted the mirror, and headed for Angel Haven. She sat at a red light, drumming her fingers on the steering wheel when a slightly familiar mental thought pattern nudged at her senses, wanting to be noticed.

She pulled off to the side of the road, sending out mental threads to follow the cry back to its source. It came again, fainter and tinged with pain. Rena grabbed the thought, and found Amy at the other end.

"*Hold on, Amy,*" she told her telepathically. "*I'm coming.*"

Rena "saw" the other men there through Amy's eyes, including Fenmore, and read the location from them. "*Hang in there, Amy. Help's on the way.*"

Rena got out of her car and found a quiet place to telekinetically change to the purple and white bodysuit she wore in her hero identity. "*Misty,*" she called. "*Amy's been picked up by Fenmore. I'm heading there now. Meet me at this address.*" She sent the location.

"*Try to get in touch with Jack. He needs to know,*" Misty sent back to her.

"*If you insist,*" Rena grumbled. Using her telekinesis, she lifted herself into the air, all the while trying to reach Jack.

A faint echo of Jack's mind resonated in her powers. "Finally," she sighed. She pulled her power in tight and punched a hole through his natural psionic shields.

"*Jack,*" she called. "*I don't care what neuroses you're currently battling over Misty being a hero. Amy's been taken by Fenmore. Meet us at this address and don't be asinine about it.*"

****

Jack paced the warehouse. Every time he thought

about Misty, he saw her tears, the hurt on her face. "I'm right," he mumbled. "I have to be or I've just made the biggest mistake of my life."

"What if you're wrong?" the little voice asked him.

Jack picked up the glass that recently held the balm to help him get through his leg repairs. He threw it against the far wall with a force usually reserved for beating the hell out of opponents and watched it disintegrate into a thousand glittering shards.

"Damn it!"

Jack felt the stirrings of telepathic contact and opened his mind, finding Rena at the other end. When she told him where Amy was and the trouble she was in, he didn't hesitate. It might be a trap, but he couldn't take the chance. He felt Rena's contempt for him linger in his mind and had a feeling she'd left it there on purpose.

"Great," he muttered. "More guilt."

Frank walked in as the bay door opened. Jack grabbed his arm. "I just had a telepathic call. Amy's been taken. We've got to go."

"Right behind you." Frank stopped long enough to grab his own arsenal before climbing in the van.

****

Misty and Rena stood where they could keep an eye on the building and not be seen by those inside.

"Can't we go in yet?" Rena asked, her voice sharp with impatience.

Misty looked up and down the road. "Not until Jack gets here."

"Well, Mr. Fancy Pants better get here toot sweet."

A sleek black van pulled up and Jack stepped out carrying his rifle and still armed to the teeth. Frank carried two auto-pistols and a combat knife strapped to his leg. They approached the two women.

"How many inside?" Jack asked in a low voice.

"Four agents plus Fenmore," Rena said, not allowing Misty to say anything. "I can shield Amy if you three take out the others."

Jack frowned and nodded. Rena watched Frank stare at her, his mouth hanging open, the same as Jack's had when Misty had introduced them. Frank took a deep breath and turned away, and Rena smiled, seeing his thoughts. She turned to the group. "Let's rock and roll."

Jack stared at the door then kicked it in. Rena moved in behind him and used her telekinesis to throw the guard near Amy across the room, banging him hard into the wall. Misty charged in behind her, heading for the closest agent. She passed through him then, from behind, stuck her hand through his neck to cut off his airway. As he dropped to the floor, she spun around, again turning ghost-like to let another agent's laser pass harmlessly through her.

Jack pulled his sonic rifle and leveled it at an agent heading toward Amy. The force of the sonic wave shredded the man's skin from his bones, leaving the bloody skeleton smoking on the floor.

Frank took off after Fenmore as he ran for the back exit. "I don't think so," he muttered. He grabbed the thin man by his jacket and dragged him back to the others. "Where do you think you're going, George? Party's not over yet."

Rena freed Amy, and Jack took her from the telepath's arms, cradling her close to his chest. As he held her, Frank hustled Fenmore over to them. Frank glanced at Amy, and in that split second, the councilman took advantage, elbowing him hard in the ribs before delivering a punch to Frank's face and sprinting for the rear door.

Rena started to follow him, but Jack stopped her. "Let him go. There'll be time to deal with him later." He held Amy tighter and smoothed her hair back. "I'm so sorry. I'm supposed to be watching your back. Every time I turn around, I'm letting you down."

"Jack," Rena called quietly. "The authorities are on their way. You'd better get scarce."

He kissed Amy's forehead, laying her carefully on the ground. He took a last look at the amount of injuries she'd sustained in the time Fenmore held her and rose to his feet.

He eyed Rena's form fitting costume. "I didn't know you had room in that getup for a radio."

She frowned at him. "Uh, hello? I talk to peoples' minds. Don't need a radio."

"Then read this, telepath," Jack said, moving closer to the two of them. "Get near my people again, and I'll shoot you where you stand. Is that clear?"

Misty looked away. "Perfectly."

Rena just smiled. "*There are a few other things in your brain that are perfectly clear too, Commander McClennan. Let me know when you want to talk,*" Rena told him telepathically. "*And you may put the fear of God into other people, but you don't scare me. Not. One. Bit.*"

He scowled at her, and she just watched him.

"Get going," she finally said, staring at him until he stomped outside.

****

Jack pulled out and headed for the warehouse. From the way Frank was watching him, he knew his friend was itching to ask him what was going on. "Spill it. What do you want to know?"

"How did Fenmore get his hands on Amy? How did he even know where she was?"

"I don't know." Jack glanced at him. "But I'm pretty sure it has something to do with the fact that those two heroes made her talk to them."

Frank chuckled. "Do you really believe that? No one makes Amy do anything she doesn't want to. She must've had a good reason for talking to them. If she trusted them, maybe they're not on the Council's take." He paused. "Maybe they could help us."

"I never want to hear you suggest anything like that to me again," Jack growled. "Is that completely understood? No hero can be trusted, especially not when they have ties to ULTRA."

"You know for a fact that the Council is a small faction and not even connected to the clean ULTRA. Have you thought any more about contacting Commander Frailer like we discussed?"

"Yes, and the answer is still no. No one in power is going to help."

"Yeah, but…"

Jack's hands tightened on the steering wheel. "I said no!"

Frank crossed his arms and stared out the window and the two men remained silent for the rest of the trip home.

Chapter Twenty

Misty gripped the pillow she was holding to her chest tighter when she heard the front door open. She relaxed a little when she heard Rena call her.

Rena stopped and rapped her knuckles quietly on the door. "Knock, knock."

"Go away, Rena," Misty mumbled. "I'm not in the mood."

Rena sat on the edge of the bed. "Too bad. You've got to talk this out. It's not good to keep it all inside." She smiled. "I'm cheaper than a shrink."

Misty rolled over. The way her eyes were burning, she knew they had to be ten times their normal size. "He said such horrible things to me about how no one cares about heroes and how he doesn't need me. I must've been crazy to think he loved me, especially after I found out how he feels about the hero community."

Rena smiled at her friend. "You still love the big jerk, don't you?"

Misty rolled back to her side. "Yes."

****

Jack made a rare return to the warehouse. His ammo was running low. Again. He was exhausted, he knew that much. His limbs ached, his head pounded, and the rest of him was running purely on instinct. "Just one night without dreams," he muttered. "Is that too much to ask?"

Frank was sitting on his bed when he walked in. Jack hesitated then headed straight to his footlocker. "What're you doing here? I told you I'd call if I needed help."

His friend just watched him. "Your face is bruised," Frank finally said. He nodded toward Jack's armor. "What's the rest of you look like?"

Jack cringed from the tone in his voice. "Pretty much the same." He reloaded his rifle, the moved to the pistol strapped to his leg.

"I thought as much. I've never seen so much damage to your armor. Do I even want to know what made that dent the size of a grapefruit right there in the middle?"

"No. It'll come out. It always does. A little paint and you won't even see the scratches. Or the dents. Or the gouge down the back."

"You're pushing your systems too hard," Frank said. "What'll you do if they fail at a crucial time?"

Jack jammed the pistol back in its holster. "Survive. It's all I know any more."

Frank stood and rested his hand on Jack's shoulder. He opened his mouth then shut it again before finally saying, "Come back safe."

Jack watched him leave. The silence pressed in on him, and he headed for his van. "Let tonight be the night I can sleep," he whispered.

****

It was past midnight when Jack rolled back up to the warehouse. He waited as the bay door slid upwards then pulled inside. He stepped out and frowned, gripping his pistol. The place should've been dark and silent, but there was a single light on and he heard music. He crept forward quietly, his fingers tightening around the pistol's butt.

"It's about time you got home," said a familiar voice.

He moved to the front of the couch and there lay Rena, reading one of the few books he still owned. He backed up a few paces. "What are you doing here? And how the bloody hell did you find me?"

"Really? You have to ask that?" She rolled her eyes and stood when he scowled. "Fine. I saw this location when I telepathically contacted you about Amy. And don't shout. It's not polite." She moved around the coffee table to stand in front of him. "I'm here to talk to you about your relationship with Misty, seeing as how you've completely screwed everything up."

He could tell from her stance and the look on her face she wasn't impressed with his armor, his temper, or with him in general. "Say your piece and leave."

She shrugged. "Okay." She pulled her arm back and laid a hard right cross to his cheek, boosting her strength with her telekinesis. She smiled as she watched his head rock back.

He grabbed her arm and twisted it out to the side. "What do you think you're doing?"

"I was trying to knock some sense into you." She telekinetically pulled his fingers from her arm. "But I was mistaken. You don't have any sense to knock in."

Jack stepped away from her, rubbing his jaw as he eyed her warily. Telepaths always made him jittery. "Why shouldn't I shoot you right now?"

Rena clenched her fists and closed her eyes. He

could see her lips moving and realized she was counting. When she reached ten, she looked at him again. "Try it and see where that rifle ends up."

He stalked to the bedroom, and Rena followed him. "Look, you idiot, why can't you just admit you were wrong? Just get the hell over yourself, and tell her you love her. I know it, and you know it. Misty is so messed up because of you, and you need to set it right."

Jack threw his rifle on the bed. "I can't, don't you understand? I'm a wanted man. The only end I see to this whole thing is with me dead or in prison. Do you think I want to bring her down to that?"

"You've ripped out her heart!" Rena shouted. "You think she'd care if you were in prison as long as you still loved her? She loves you, and I have no idea why!"

There it was again. That weird ability to make people shout. He had no idea why Misty still loved him, either. He threw his sword on the bed next to the rifle, took off his knife and pistol and began removing his body armor.

"I want to tell her everything she wants to hear," he murmured. "It's just impossible. Every time I go out, something else inside me breaks. One day, I'll slow down, and that'll be the end. I couldn't do that to her."

He lifted his head and looked around him. "There used to be so much more to my life. I had a house in the suburbs, a wonderful wife." He paused. "Love." He turned to Rena. "I was actually human then." He pulled at the synthetic skin on his arm. "I'm more machine than man these days. With everything that's happened, everything I've done, it's put me on a long road to nowhere."

"I've seen in your mind what you've been through,

and no one should ever have to endure all that." She stepped closer to him. "Let her help you. You have to let the healing begin sometime. You've already let pain and anger fester in you for thirteen long years. Let it go. Find that part of you that still loves, that still trusts, and give it to Misty. You won't be sorry."

Jack considered her words. Did he still have that small part that believed? "How do I know you're not telepathically influencing me?"

She laid her hand on his arm. "If I was in your noggin, you'd know." She smiled. "At least think about it."

Jack stared at her, before slowly nodding. "I'll think about it."

Rena blew out a breath. "I'll take it." She headed for the door. "And Jack, you're not the only one to doubt their humanity. At least you started human. I still don't know what I am." She waved over her shoulder. "See you around, field commander."

****

Jack stored his gear and sat on the couch, drinking his last beer. Rena's words stayed with him as he slowly savored the cold brew in his hands. "Trust," he murmured. "Can I still trust?"

He thought about his wife, and then Misty. He'd trusted Carol completely in their days at ULTRA. He'd even trusted Misty in some pretty serious situations. He went to his desk and pulled out Carol's picture. Sitting back down, he traced her face with his finger.

His chest grew tight, and his eyes burned. He laid his head back, pictures of the past flooding his mind no matter how hard he tried to banish them.

Frank and Amy dropped him off at the corner and

took off, just like he told them to. He ran for his house and grabbed Carol as she waited for him on the porch.

"We've got to get out of here," he told her.

Carol shook her head. "They're on to you. They knew you were coming."

"That's right," Fenmore said as he appeared behind her with a gun pointed at them. "Inside."

Jack gazed at his wife. "It'll be all right. Don't worry."

The agents forced them inside, and Jack was pushed into a chair. Donald Harrington walked out of the dining room. Jack watched him as he stood there, staring down.

"Well, Jackie boy, you've stirred up quite the hornets' nest," he said, smiling an oily grimace that made Jack's skin crawl. "Just tell us what we want to know, and the two of you will get out of this without a scratch."

Jack eyed the gun in Harrington's shoulder holster. "No scratches," he said. "Just a couple of bullet holes."

Harrington folded his hands. "We just want what evidence you've gathered, and to know who you've told. You're a good agent." He looked at Carol then back. "Maybe a little too good. Just tell us everything, and you'll be free to go."

Jack stared up at him. "Now, why don't I believe you?"

Fenmore stepped forward. "It's true. The Council doesn't want any more trouble than necessary. Give us the information, and you're done with us."

Jack was silent as he watched Fenmore walk over to Carol and pull her to her feet.

"Surely, you're prepared to be sensible," he said. He nodded to an agent who pulled a long knife from his boot. "Open him up."

The agent ripped the knife down Jack's arm, making him cry out. Fenmore smiled as he watched Jack's blood well and drip on the carpet.

"Tell us what we want to know, or I'll have him gutted," Fenmore said. They moved in again, and Carol cried out.

"I don't know anything. Jack hasn't told anyone what information he has. No one knows where it is." She grabbed Fenmore's jacket. "Please, don't hurt him."

Jack watched his enemies. He scanned the room and knew it was now or never. He sprung from the chair, driving his fist into the knife wielder's face. He blocked a punch from a man behind him and saw Carol take out Harrington from the corner of his eye. They made it to the front door, when a bullet ripped through his leg, dropping him to one knee.

"Carol, get out of here."

She pulled him to his feet. "Not without you."

The agents jumped them, and they were brought back to the living room where Jack was, again, shoved into the chair, and Carol was held by Harrington.

Fenmore glared at him. "That was inconvenient. Now, Jack, is what she said true?"

Jack felt warm blood run down his leg and watched more drip from his fingers. Fenmore backhanded him. "Answer me."

Jack nodded. "It's true. No one knows but me."

"Where's the evidence?" Fenmore turned the gun to Carol. "Don't make me ask again."

"Carol, I'm sorry," Jack whispered.

She smiled at him, and he could see in her eyes that she knew what was coming. "It's all right. Just tell them, and then everything will be all right."

Fenmore hit him again, and Jack felt his lip split. "You're wasting time."

"It's in my office at ULTRA," he said. "Let her go."

Fenmore smiled. "Thank you, Jack. That wasn't so hard, was it?" He pointed the gun at Carol. "But loose ends cannot be left hanging." And he pulled the trigger, filling the room with the acrid stink of gunpowder, and Carol jerked backwards.

Jack surged out of the chair. "No!" he screamed, hitting everyone in his path.

He grabbed Carol and held her close as her blood soaked through his clothes and covered his hands. Tears streamed down his face as he screamed her name, again and again and again.

Something hit the back of his head, and that was all he knew until he awoke in jail.

Jack rubbed his eyes, trying to focus on the present. That same scene had been his constant companion for thirteen years. He'd sat there helpless while his wife was murdered. He was supposed to protect her. He was, after all, one of the good guys. A hero. He frowned. He hated that word and everything that went with it. As far as he was concerned, the whole hero population could go straight to hell.

But now, he had Misty, and she was one of them. She was not only a hero, but an ULTRA liaison. The two things he hated most in one beautiful, selfless woman. She knew all about him and still wanted to help him. All she asked for was his trust, but he hadn't trusted heroes in a long time.

"I don't think I can change," he whispered as darkness began to fill the warehouse.

Chapter Twenty-One

George sat behind his desk, staring at Donald. He was beginning to regret bringing him in. If it wasn't for the other man's ties with the Leaders, he'd get rid of him and do the job himself. Donald had told him about his encounter with the maid in exceedingly graphic detail, like he'd wanted to know.

"You're having no better luck than I am," Fenmore said quietly.

Harrington smoothed his pants. "You think I don't know that? We should pick up the woman he's been seen with lately. If that doesn't bring him out in the open, nothing will."

"Bring her here." Fenmore leaned forward. "And this time, don't get sidetracked."

Harrington narrowed his eyes and nodded once. "When everything's over, George, I'll do as I please with her."

****

The afternoon sun was covered by fluffy white clouds as Jack prowled the streets, his armor feeling like it weighed more than usual. He had paced the warehouse one too many times, stared at the phone, one too many times. He'd almost gotten himself under control when Rena showed up and started all those disturbing thoughts all over again. Taking to the streets seemed the best course of action.

He saw his informant shuffle by. Talking to someone, anyone, would help. He leaped off the building, landing behind the street man as he turned down the alley.

"Evening, Mexico."

Mexico, jumped, then smiled, seeing who said his name. He straightened up and lost the heavy Spanish accent he used around everyone else. "Hey, Jack. What brings you this way tonight?"

Jack shrugged. "Not much. Didn't feel like sitting home. Heard anything new?"

Mexico shook his head. "Not a peep. It's not like ULTRA to suddenly clam up. Fenmore's crowd is probably planning something big. Watch your back, boss. I don't like the way things feel these days."

"I know what you mean." Jack looked around, almost feeling the city hold its breath, as if it knew something bad was coming. He handed a wad of bills to Mexico. "Here. How much longer are you going to be sponging off me?"

The Hispanic man grinned. "As long as you're paying the bills, I see this going on for a long time." As he took the money, the edge of tattoo peeked out from his jacket cuff on his wrist.

Jack grabbed his arm, pushing the sleeve up and smiled. "The old Gravedigger emblem. I'd almost forgotten what it looked like. You know, if anyone recognizes that, you're a dead man."

"Live on the edge or not at all," Mexico said. "Isn't that what we used to say?"

Jack nodded. "Yeah, but this edge is getting sharper all the time. Be careful."

Mexico grabbed him in a tight hug. Stepping back,

he gripped his friend's shoulders. "You too, Jack."

****

Misty and Rena walked back to Misty's apartment. Rena glanced at her. "Will you be okay?"

Misty nodded. "I'll be fine. Go back to the mansion."

"Hey. I know he loves you. Hold on to that."

Misty nodded again, unlocking her apartment as her friend headed toward the elevators. She wandered through her home, seeing him everywhere. He sat there, on her couch. He held her there, by the door. She couldn't even look at the bedroom, remembering the passion they'd shared.

Misty went to the kitchen, taking out things to make something to eat, then putting them back. She walked back out to the living room and sank down on the couch, clutching a throw pillow to her chest. "Damn you, Jack McClennan. I love you."

"That's just what I wanted to hear." Harrington stepped out of the darkness, flanked by two agents.

Misty shot to her feet. *Why didn't Rena sense them?* "What do you want?"

Harrington folded his arms while he looked her over. "We're taking you to ULTRA. Our ULTRA."

Misty walked around the couch to be in a better position to defend herself. "I don't think so. I know who you are and I know what you've done." Misty engaged her power and stuck her intangible hand into the windpipe of the nearest agent and partially solidified, cutting off his air.

A laser passed through her and she turned, coming back to the solid plane and hitting the agent who fired with an open palm strike before he could re-calibrate his weapon. She was turning desolid again when Harrington's voice stopped her.

"You wouldn't think of leaving, would you?" He opened her front door, and an agent came in, carrying Rena's unconscious form. "I would hate for anything to happen to your friend."

Misty's chest grew tight as icy fingers clamped around her heart. She couldn't draw a decent breath to loosen the chill that gripped her. If they decided to kill Rena, she wouldn't be able to stop them. She lifted her gaze to Harrington. "You win," she growled. "But if you hurt her, you'll regret it."

Harrington smiled. "I knew you'd see it my way. Drop her and let's go."

The agent dumped Rena on the floor and, as they stepped over her, Misty tried to see if she was all right as she was shoved out the door and herded into a waiting van.

****

Misty was locked in a barren, white room. She paced the confines, stopping every few steps to glare at the door. In a weird way, she missed all the usual interrogation items. There should've been a two-way mirror, a metal table with spindly legs, and at least two uncomfortable chairs.

When Harrington said "our ULTRA" she had a feeling she wouldn't be seeing the usual agents walking around. She definitely knew she wouldn't come across Commander Frailer. She sighed. However, she wasn't expecting to be dumped in a room and left alone for who knew how long.

She glanced at the door again. "What the heck are they waiting for?"

The door opened and a thin man with small round glasses and wearing an expensive suit walked in. He was the ULTRA psychologist that had been on the newscast and also the man from the restaurant when she and Rena had spoken to Amy. "Good evening, miss. I'm George Fenmore. Please tell me what you know about Jack McClennan."

Misty stared at him. Fluorescent light was definitely not kind to him. It showed the pallor of his skin, the wrinkles on his face. "According to your interview on NewsLine, you used to work with him and were friends. Shouldn't you know everything by now?"

He stepped closer to her. "Don't try my patience. Just tell me where he is and you can go."

Misty backed away from him, the strong smell of his over-used cologne making her want to gag. "I don't know where he is right now. He always came for me. I don't know where he lives."

"That's unfortunate." Fenmore checked his watch. "I have another appointment. I'll be back later to continue this discussion."

"Don't do me any favors," she mumbled as he walked out.

Misty tried to trigger her desolidification, but couldn't get her power to work. She examined the room and noticed small round devices set into the ceiling at each corner. As lights flashed when she tried to activate her powers, she knew exactly what they were. "Stupid power inhibitors," she grumbled.

She sat down. One thing left to try. Hopefully, she could get a telepathic message out. She refused to consider that Rena wasn't in a state to hear her down the link they shared. She crossed her fingers and, steadying her breathing, sent a message to her friend. "Please hear me, Red," she whispered.

Chapter Twenty-Two

"I must be alive," Rena mumbled. "I hurt too much to be dead."

She groaned and pushed herself up. The pounding in her skull matched the flip-flopping her stomach was doing every time she moved. She closed her eyes, cradling her head.

"Psychic shields should be against the law." She rubbed the back of her neck. The pounding continued, and it finally dawned on her that someone was at the door.

Rena staggered over and threw it open. Seeing Jack, she frowned. "Just what I need. Of all the people to drop by, it had to be Mr. Congeniality."

Jack walked in, closing the door as he watched Rena walk to the couch. "What's wrong? Where's Misty?"

"I don't know," Rena mumbled as she continued to hold her head.

He sat next to her. "What do you mean, 'you don't know'?"

"I mean those imbeciles you're mixed up with took her, you idiot!" Rena shouted, realizing too late, that was a mistake. She groaned and massaged her temples.

"Bloody hell." He got up and began to pace. "How long ago?"

"I don't know," Rena said, looking up at him.

"They ambushed me in the hall and shot me with something. I couldn't detect them. Now, I've got a screaming headache and my body feels like it weighs two tons."

Jack knelt in front of her and turned her head left and right, studying her eyes. "Looks like they got you with one of the more powerful neural sedatives. You'll be all right."

Rena frowned at him. "I feel like hell. Give me a minute. I should be able to at least ease the pain."

Jack nodded and stood. "I'll ask around downstairs. The longer they have her..."

"Don't think like that." Rena said, interrupting him. "She'll be fine. Even if she can't use her powers, she's not powerless. Go. I'll be good in a few minutes."

Jack came back in just as Rena sat back. "They left a couple of hours ago."

A couple of hours? Rena thought. "How much sedative did they hit me with?" She looked at her watch. It was after seven. It would be getting close to being dark out.

"Let me try mind scanning for her," Rena said. "Our team has a permanent telepathic link between us. I should be able to pick her up if they haven't psychically shielded her."

Jack nodded. "Go for it."

Rena opened her mind. *I should not be doing this so soon after a headache*, she thought. But even that wouldn't stop her from trying to find her friend.

After several long, tense minutes, she looked up at him. "That's that."

"Did you find her?" he asked, staring at her.

Rena shook her head. "No. But there's a huge

psychic blanket over one particular area of the city. I suggest we start there." He looked at her, and she grinned. "A psychic shield would have to be really powerful to cut me off so completely from any member of the Angels."

Jack smiled. "And if you were a secret cabal hidden within a highly respected organization, you wouldn't want stray telepaths locking in on you."

She pointed at him. "Bingo." She stood and went to the door. "Let's boogie."

****

"Their evil plan is to make me crack from super boredom," Misty said. At first, she jumped at every sound, real and imagined. As nothing happened, she paced. She tired of that and sat. Now, she just wanted them to do something before she lost her mind.

She sat cross-legged in the middle of the floor and watched the door. Soon she rested her chin on her hands. She stretched her legs out, bracing herself with her arms. After a few minutes, she stood back up and resumed her pacing, all the while, keeping an eye on the door. She kept expecting it to open and some strange, mad scientist to come in with bizarre machines that were actually torture devices. She smiled. Definitely too many late night bad horror movies.

She kept trying to reach Rena but got no response. It's due to a psychic shield, she told herself. Nothing more. Rena was fine. She'd find her. In the meantime, she kept trying to communicate with her friend.

The door opened, and Misty jumped as the imagined sound was finally real. Fenmore walked in, and she faced him, straightening her spine and ready for whatever he decided to do. "What now?" she demanded.

"I thought we could continue our conversation in my office," he said, gesturing toward the open door.

That was unexpected, and she was tempted to refuse, but staring at the blank, white walls was making her nuts. She clenched her fists as Fenmore escorted her to his office. Misty stared at him as she sat in the firm chair.

"*Rena, if you can hear me, now would be a good time to say something,*" Misty said telepathically.

****

Rena stood in Jack's warehouse, tapping her foot with impatience as he finished donning his armor and making sure his weapons were loaded and fully primed. By the time they made it there, the sun had gone down and stars lit the sky. She halted, feeling Misty's mind connect with hers.

"*Rena, if you can hear me, now would be a good time to say something.*"

"*Misty!*" she cried, her mind's voice flooded with relief. "*Where are you? You scared the hell out of me!*"

"*Payback, Red, for making me think they cut short your very interesting life,*" Misty replied. "*I'm not sure exactly where I'm at. It could be near ULTRA's headquarters. I know how much time it takes to get there from my apartment and it was about the same amount.*"

Rena grinned. "*I've got a fix on you now, kid. It doesn't matter how they try to hide you. I know where you are and when I get there, I'll be all over them like ugly on an ape.*"

Misty's mental voice held a frown. "*Do you have to use such childish phrases all the time?*"

"Of course. It adds color to my repertoire," Rena grinned. *"Got to go. See you soon."*

Misty hesitated for a moment. *"Make sure you don't tell Jack. I'm being used as bait for some kind of trap. Bring anyone else, but not him."*

"It's okay," Rena said. *"I've got everything under control."*

Rena broke contact and saw Jack staring at her. She held her hands up. "Misty's fine. That was her on the mental telephone. I didn't pick up that she'd been hurt or messed with in any way. She says they're waiting for you, and she's some kind of bait."

Jack ran his hands through his hair. "And they couldn't have picked a better bait." He looked at Rena. "I told her being with me was dangerous. Could you see where she was being held?"

"Not really." She winked. "But I got the sense it was in the same area as the psychic shield. I am just too good."

Jack frowned. "Can't you be serious for one minute?"

She pinched his cheek. "Can't you lighten up?" She telekinetically changed to her hero outfit. "Let's go."

$$****$$

Jack had to stop himself from speeding to get to Misty. He saw Rena out of the corner of his eye watching the city pass by as the van quietly hummed.

"You have a voice recognition program, thumb print scanner, and at least three different security locks on this thing," she finally said. "There're women who don't get this much attention."

"This van cost a lot to outfit," Jack muttered.

She grinned. "Misty's cheaper."

"One more word and you walk, *understand*?"

"A lot more than you think."

Jack glanced at her. "I don't get you. I've worked with telepaths in the past, and they're nothing like you."

"What do you mean?"

He shrugged. "They held themselves apart from the rest of the team. They acted like they were better than the rest of us. They were cold and condescending. You're nothing like that. Why?"

She shifted in the seat. "I have a twin sister. She manipulates light." She paused. "When we were growing up, she was in my mind all the time. Our psychic rapport was deeper and stronger than regular human twins. When we were teenagers, we were picked up by HelixCorp. Our psychic bond limited our abilities, and they destroyed it. Nara told me not to hold myself apart from people. She said I needed them. Then, her powers drove her crazy."

Jack sat silently. What had the telepath been through in her life? His lips tightened, and he glanced at her again. She looked sad, like she was thinking about things best forgotten.

"We did some bad things," Rena continued. "Then, I went to the Angels for help. My powers are out of control. Misty has always been there for me." She sat up a little straighter and the familiar grin was back. "So now, I'm going to get her out of there and kick all kinds of butt while I'm at it."

"What exactly are you capable of?" Jack asked her quietly.

Rena shook her head. "You don't want to know." Her gaze narrowed. "Stop here."

Chapter Twenty-Three

Jack wasn't surprised to find the ULTRA Headquarters building as their destination. Fenmore's crowd hung out in secret sublevels of the massive structure. "Scan the building."

Rena mind scanned the whole area, not just the looming edifice in front of them. "No psychic shield. You think they were expecting us this soon?"

They stepped out of the van, and Jack grabbed his rifle. "It's a safe bet. They'd want us to find her quickly to trap me. In the back, there's a hidden door there that the clean ULTRA doesn't know about. That's where we go in."

She stared at him. "And you're privy to this information how?"

He smiled. "It pays to know you're enemy."

She laid her hand on his arm. "Do you want me to contact the ULTRA commander? I know he'd believe you, and he could help."

"One step at a time, Red."

She chuckled. "Misty calls me that. You guys are so suited."

"Can you focus on getting her out?" Jack sighed.

She punched his shoulder lightly. "You are such an old lady."

He slowly grinned. He'd never been accused of acting like an old lady before. "Okay, Rena. Ready?"

She nodded and he led her to the back of the building.

He pulled a key card from his belt and slid it through the slot. A green light blinked as the door swung quietly inward. "I 'borrowed' this from one of their operatives when I came for my armor. I checked the layout before I left, but I've never had the chance to use it since. I'm surprised it still works."

"You've had it all these years, and you've never used it or got around to returning it?" Rena asked.

"Nope."

"Remind me never to loan you a library book."

Jack hesitated. "Are you sure you want to do this?"

She nodded. "My best friend is in there. So, yes. I'm positive I want to do this."

****

A light on top of Fenmore's desk began to blink, and he smiled as he raised his eyes to Misty. "He's right on time."

Misty tried to ignore the armed guards behind her and glared at Fenmore. "Who's right on time?"

Fenmore looked at her, confusion on his face. "Why, your stalwart hero. He's coming to save you from our evil clutches. I'm surprised you wouldn't know that."

It couldn't be him. Misty knew there'd been no contact between the two of them since Amy's rescue. "It could be anyone up there."

Fenmore shook his head. "No. It could only be Jack. He stole a key card, and we activated the tracer programmed into it so that if he ever came back here, we'd be alerted."

Rena, if you told him, you are so dead. Misty just stared at Fenmore, not wanting to give him the reaction he wanted.

"Now, after all we've talked about, I'm sure you can see his guilt for yourself," Fenmore said as he folded his hands on his desk.

Misty leaned forward in the chair. "The only thing I'm sure of is his innocence."

Fenmore laughed. "You're not using your head. He *is* guilty. I've personally seen to that."

****

"Misty's below us," Rena said quietly. She stared at the hallway stretching before them and knew there must be more to the hidden area. "How far down does the bad guys' lair go?"

Jack shrugged as he took the first few steps in. "I'm not sure. I wasn't able to penetrate too far into their HQ. It can't go too far down. That much activity would be noticed no matter how hard they'd try to hide it."

Rena looked up at him. "I haven't been able to detect any other thought patterns either. They're more than likely shielded. From the strength of the shield I detected earlier, their armor is probably patched into somehow. And I couldn't sense them when they jumped me at Misty's place."

"Or because they're trying to grab me, it's most likely the trap we think it is." He glanced at her. "Either way, it wouldn't exactly be over populated now, would it?"

"I guess not," Rena said. "But to feel a place this empty gives me some serious heebie jeebies."

"Most of my missions are like this."

"Thanks. I feel so much better."

Jack glanced at her. "You could always join my

team. Do this enough and it'll cure your heebie jeebies."

She tapped her chin. "Um, I don't think so."

They hurried to the end of the long corridor ahead of them, passing several doors to each side of them before stopping at the final door on their right. Jack eased it open and they headed down the dimly lit staircase. At the third floor, Rena put her hand on Jack's arm.

He looked back at her. "What?"

"I'm picking up someone." She paused. "It's Misty."

"Rena, go back. They think Jack is up there, and they've set some kind of a trap."

"It's okay. We know what we're doing," Rena told her.

"What do you mean 'we'?" Misty asked her cautiously.

Rena glanced at her partner. *"He's big, has red hair, and is not as much of a jerk as I originally thought."*

"What were the two of you thinking?" Misty's mental voice shouted. *"And why did you tell him where I was?"*

Rena shrugged. *"He was there the first time you contacted me. And you try and leave him behind and see how far you get. See you soon."*

Jack looked at her. "Well?"

Rena grinned. "She's pissed you're here."

"She can't have everything her way."

Rena nodded, still smiling. She tried scanning again, but even with the shield down, her mind felt fuzzy. She thought she detected someone on the floor they stood on.

"Hold it. I think someone's here."

They started down the hallway, trusting Jack's augmented hearing more than Rena's telepathy. With the psychic shield up, they couldn't be sure if she could detect someone before they were ambushed. They paused before a door halfway down and Jack kicked the door open.

Inside, a teenage girl sat huddled on the bed, arms were wrapped around her legs. She wore a brown and blue bodysuit and had her long, black hair was pulled up, allowing them to see the sadness that filled her large gray eyes.

"I'm so sorry," she said.

Jack sat next to her. "For what?"

She closed her eyes as she turned her head away. "For tracking you. For always leading them to you. I tried to allow enough time for you to escape."

He took her hand. "You're much too young to be involved with something like this."

She looked at him. "I had to co-operate with them. They'd send me back to HelixCorp if I didn't."

Rena shuddered. "I understand exactly what you mean. You're the next phase in HelixCorp's psionic program, aren't you?"

The girl nodded. "I've been code named Mindspell. I don't even remember my real name any more."

Jack raised her face to his. "Do you know where Misty is?"

"She's in Fenmore's office on the fifth floor. It's the lowest and most secure level. He's been preparing for your arrival ever since she was brought here."

Jack took her hands. "Thank you."

"I'll try to mask your presence from them as long as I can." She looked at Rena. "I know the holes in their shielding. I won't be able to move from here. I'll need to maintain my focus."

"I'll come back for you. I promise."

Mindspell smiled a little at Jack. "I'll be waiting."

They headed back to the stairwell, Jack's stride sure and purposeful. "I didn't think they'd resort to abusing a young girl."

"If she's from HelixCorp, she's been through worse," Rena muttered. She felt Jack's stare and his mind told her that he was wondering about her past.

"Let's get Misty," he said. "Then we'll tie up the loose ends."

Rena nodded, and they set off at a determined trot.

****

The door crashed open, and Fenmore shot to his feet as Misty snapped around in her chair. Jack stood there, his rifle in his right hand, Rena behind him. Anger etched itself into every line of his face, but this time, it was directed at the man behind the desk.

"Let her go," Jack growled.

Fenmore walked around to the front of the desk and leaned against it. "It's been a long time since I last saw you in ULTRA armor."

Jack scowled at him. "I'm only going to tell you one more time. Let her go."

Fenmore just smiled and gestured the guards back. He looked at Misty. "Get out."

Misty frowned. This was a little too easy. "What do you get out of this, Fenmore?"

He folded his arms and looked straight at Jack. "Nothing in life is free." He turned to Rena. "You get her. I get him."

Jack raised the rifle. "What makes you think I won't kill you and leave?"

Fenmore nodded to the doorway. At least ten agents had filed in behind them.

"*Stupid psychic shields,*" Rena mentally told both her partners.

"I'll have the two of them cut to ribbons before your eyes." He smiled. "Just like the old days. Remember those prototype guns? Here they are. First they shut down a 'super's' powers, then they shut down the 'super'."

Misty saw Rena look at Jack, and he waved her silent.

"Deal," was all he said.

Misty ran to him. "You can't do it," she begged. "I won't let you."

Jack glared at Fenmore. "I want to see them leave the building, not just your assurance."

Fenmore nodded once. "I think that's reasonable. Let's take them out now. You and I have a lot to discuss."

At the outside door, Rena and Jack had just come in, Fenmore moved in front of them. "Don't try and tell anyone about this place. They won't believe you, and even if they do, we have measures in place to assure our security. All you'll end up doing is looking like fools. After all, Commander Michael Frailer put me in charge of apprehending McClennan. I'm just doing my job."

Misty turned and looked at Jack. He gave her a slight shake of his head. She turned to Rena, who shrugged. If Jack didn't want her in his mind, she wasn't getting in.

"Move it." Two of the guards gave them a shove away from the building.

Rena tugged at Misty's arm. "Come on."

Misty frowned as Rena dragged her away. "What's going on, Red? I've never seen you run from a fight before."

Rena stayed silent all the way back to Jack's van.

Chapter Twenty-Four

Jack had parked at the far end of the parking lot where there was very little light. Rena understood why, but now it was downright creepy with the shadows getting longer and the rustle of leaves in the slight summer breeze. She stared at the van. Having seen what Jack went through to get it open, she knew that wasn't going to happen for her.

"Somebody better show up soon," she grumbled. "I don't want to stand out here all night."

"Rena, please," Misty said, staring back at the building they'd just left. "Jack's in serious trouble. He probably won't live through what they'll do to him. We've got get back in there."

Rena let out a short, piercing scream. "Between the two of you, I'm going to be in therapy for the rest of my life!" She threw her hands in the air, walking a couple of steps away before turning around. "Didn't you think I'd expect him to do something this stupid?" She slammed her fist against the side of the van. "Didn't you think I'd have a back-up plan in case he pulled a stunt like this? It's the first thing the Angels taught me. Always have a back-up plan."

She stalked to the front of the van and then back. "Jack's expecting to die in there. You're expecting him to die in there." She held her hands up stopping anything Misty might say. "Don't say it. It's in your head. A head, I might add, I'm seriously considering knocking off your fool shoulders!" she shouted. She balled her fists in a supreme effort not to shake Misty senseless. "I don't intend to let that happen."

Misty stepped back. "You wanted him locked away. Why the change of heart?"

Rena folded her arms. "Because when you get stuck with someone, you get a feel for their personality. Jack's way too bitter and holds too much grief inside to be guilty of what they claim he did." She finally smiled. "He's a good man."

"Your telepathy tell you that?"

Rena grinned and nodded. "Yep. And I'm tired of babysitting him. Take him back, please."

Misty smiled a little. "So, since you seem to have all the answers, what's the plan?"

"I telepathically called Captain Starblast before we came here." Rena leaned against the van. "Kristin sent the rest of the Angels to Russia for some heavy political thing, and they'd never make it back in time." She looked up at Misty. "I want to see Michael Frailer, the head of ULTRA."

Misty grinned. "Sounds like a plan. Let's go."

****

Misty paced and stared down the road every couple of minutes. "Remember how badly Amy was worked over in the short amount of time she was held?"

Rena nodded.

"Jack will go through worse because he's their actual target. So, the sooner we get back there, the better."

Rena stared at her friend, not a trace of her usual humor in her face.

They both turned as a black SUV pulled up next to them. Captain Starblast emerged and walked over to them.

He laid his hand on Misty's shoulder. "This time, things will be set right."

Misty couldn't help feeling confident at his words. She nodded, not trusting herself to say anything without bursting into tears.

The captain turned to Rena. "Rena, you said you wanted to see Commander Frailer?"

She nodded. "Yes. He needs to be brought in the loop. We can't do this without him. I tried to get Jack to call him, but he wouldn't do it. Redheads really are stubborn."

Cap nodded once. "Let's go."

Rena used her telekinesis to change Misty's street clothes into her yellow and white hero outfit and handed her the white domino mask. "You might need this."

She took it and smiled. "Thanks, Rena."

The two Angels hurried after Captain Starblast as he strode into ULTRA's building.

****

Jack was escorted into a solid white barren room. He inhaled deeply. He could smell Misty's perfume, but whether she had been here or he was just wishing, he didn't know. He turned, facing Fenmore and his squad.

Fenmore looked him up and down. "You're a disgrace to that armor. Take it off."

"Make me," Jack growled.

Fenmore turned to the squad leader. "I'll be back in fifteen minutes. Ensure his co-operation."

The squad leader approached Jack. "Easy or hard?"

Jack grinned, rolling his shoulders. "Hard." He pulled back his arm and let fly with a haymaker, landing squarely on the man's chin. The leader's helmet stopped the force of the blow. *Bloody hell. Is everyone augmented these days?*

The agents circled him and he anticipated their coordinated attack. Bring it on, he thought.

The agents jumped him simultaneously and held him. Jack pulled against their holds, but the damned augmented armor stopped him. They yanked his gauntlets off and his breastplate followed. He got an arm free to punch the man on his right, and then he got clouted in the back of his head. Struck a few more times, he fell to his knees.

I guess they can make me, he thought.

****

Jack smiled slightly at Fenmore's surprised look when he came back. The Council's squad didn't fare so well against him. One man was dead, his head tilted at an unnatural angle, and the rest of the team were strewn about the room, breathing, but not moving. Jack had been stripped of his gear and was standing in the center of the room in just his underwear as the squad leader covered him from a safe distance.

Fenmore smiled. "It's nice to see you still have some life left in you. If you'd just given up, I'd have been very disappointed."

Jack frowned. "Well, we wouldn't want that now, would we?"

Fenmore turned as his partner, Harrington, entered. "He's as defiant as ever," Fenmore said.

"I suspected he would be." Harrington glanced at him. "I've notified the Leaders he's in our custody.

They're very pleased with us."

Jack just stared at both men. "What do the two of you want?"

Harrington sauntered over to him and leaned close. "Payback. You lied to us, Jack, and that wasn't nice of you. The evidence was never in your office. Very unprofessional, my friend. Yet, it proves you were a liar even back then."

Jack just stared at them. They'd never found the files and pictures he'd gathered so carefully over two long years. That evidence could've stopped Fenmore all those long years ago. He'd had his fingers in every crime that was listed from selling classified information to black market arms dealing. He'd hidden it so only he and his team knew where its location. It would've shaken ULTRA to its very core. So many people were involved. He frowned. And so many of his team were dead because of it.

"So, what's your point?" Jack asked.

Harrington shook his head. "We had to ask one of your own team. He liked the money we gave him and took us right to where it was really hidden."

Jack's hands balled. Betrayed by someone on his team. His eyes narrowed, and his shallow breathing signaled his anger began a slow burn.

"Keep that famous temper of yours in check," Harrington said. "Your people took care of who they considered a traitor a long time ago."

Sure, Jack thought. *That's why Frank and Amy were so evasive about how Captain Starblast ended up with doctored evidence.* He could almost see his team carrying out their own justice for the crime of betraying their field commander. They had probably executed the sell-out as soon as they had found him.

Fenmore laughed. "I wish I could've seen your face when Captain Starblast showed up with what you thought was *your* evidence. I was told you were so angry, you threatened to kill him."

Jack remembered the whole thing. Turned out, the captain hadn't betrayed him after all. He got played as hard as everyone connected with this case. *Does Cap know any of this?* he wondered.

"So you sent Captain Starblast to the prison with your fake evidence. Did you keep the originals or were you smart enough to destroy them?"

Harrington moved back toward the door. "The Council has it in a safe place. It's a constant reminder they shouldn't slip up again. I'm not at liberty to tell you the location. You understand our need for secrecy, right?"

Jack snorted. "Why do you think I'd give a damn about your needs?"

"After all these years, your answers are still predictable." Fenmore stood to the side and ordered a new squad into the room. "Give him the works. If he's still on his feet when we return, it will be you who answer to the Leaders for your failure."

Harrington looked at Jack. "There'll be a telepath coming. I don't know what she has planned, but I hope it hurts."

****

ULTRA Commander Michael Frailer had just gotten back into his office when Cap, Misty, and Rena entered.

"Your call caught me just before I left for the night," Mike said. "You said you had some new evidence about a long standing case. What can I help you with?"

"Scavenger, also known as Jack McClennan," was all the captain said, and Michael visibly cringed.

The commander squeezed his eyes shut. "That man has been a thorn in the side of this organization and myself for years."

"I know, Michael," Cap said. "Right now, Jack McClennan needs our help. Remember back when he insisted there were other people involved with what he'd been accused of? Well, he was right. There's a secret cabal in ULTRA. They call themselves The Council. They're the ones directly responsible for Jack being a thorn in your side."

"This is the first I've heard of this 'Council.' What exactly is it?"

Misty pushed her way forward, stopping Cap from saying anything. "We don't have time to tell you everything right now. The people holding him now are the ones truly responsible for a lot of the things Jack was accused of. Just promise me, when we get him back you'll hear him out before doing anything."

"I don't know if I can do that. He's a wanted felon."

Misty leaned close to Mike. "Please, promise me!"

Captain Starblast laid his hand on Misty's shoulder. "I'll take full responsibility for him."

"Jack McClennan is no more a bad guy than you," Rena said. "We just want to know you'll be open minded."

Mike hesitated, then nodded. "Find him. Secure him. Let me know when he's safe."

Misty stood back, breathing a sigh of relief. "Sure

thing, Commander Frailer."

As the trio left the office, Rena turned to her friend. "Begging now? I never thought I'd see the day. It has to be true love. Jack has really got you tied up in knots."

Chapter Twenty-Five

The door shut, and the automatic lock shot home as Jack watched the four agents plus the squad leader advance on him. He wasn't leaving here, at least not on his feet. Everything he and his team had worked for was coming to an end, but not the end he'd hoped.

Anger rose, hot and molten inside him, and for the first time in years, he let it. It was his oldest and best friend, giving him strength to deal with bad situations, giving him power when he needed it most. He grinned. Oh, he expected to go to hell. He just didn't think he'd have this much company.

Two agents rushed him. He grabbed the one on his left and swung him around into the one on his right. As he did, he was struck in the back, by a third, the impact knocking him to his knees. He pushed himself up, struggling to get his breath back.

He rammed his elbow straight back, feeling it connect with his opponent. It drove the agent off balance, but Jack doubted it did any real damage. If he'd been in his own armor, things would be different. His gear lay piled in a far corner of the room, and there was no way they were going to let him get to it.

He'd checked the agents when they first entered, but none carried a weapon. So much for the idea of grabbing a sidearm and escaping. An armored fist drove into his stomach, dropping him again to the floor. *I'm beginning to hate augmented armor.*

The squad leader stepped forward. "You're good, McClennan. Shame we couldn't have worked together."

Jack scowled at him. "As long as your loyalties lie with these people, the chances of us ever working together are nil."

The leader chuckled. "They're nil anyway because you're not leaving here."

Jack lunged forward, tackling the man in front of him. He slammed the man's head against the floor, hoping at least to stun him for a few seconds. Hands pulled him off and threw him against the far wall. As an agent swung at his head, Jack dropped, taking the man out with a leg sweep.

The squad leader walked over and grabbed Jack by his hair, pulling him to his feet. "You're making this too easy, renegade."

He twisted free of the man's grip, feeling his scalp tear as he left the agent with a handful of red hair. Blood trickled down his face. "Then allow me to up the stakes."

Jack grabbed a rushing agent and slammed him into the squad leader, taking both men down. Another agent came up on his right, surprising him with a kidney punch, then kicked out his right knee. With no armor to block the hit, Jack crumpled to the floor. The agents descended on him, their armored fists doing more damage than he thought possible.

"Enough," came a commanding voice from the doorway.

The agents turned to see a blonde woman standing there. Her psionic ability radiated out from her, making the agents instinctively back away, knowing they wanted no part of her. She wore small, round glasses that accentuated the hate in her eyes.

"When I am done with this first session, you may have whatever is left of him, Squad Leader."

The leader bowed and stepped away from Jack. "Whatever you want."

She stood over Jack and frowned. "Get up," she demanded. "I want to see you when you break."

Jack spit blood on the floor. The Council agents were good and stronger than he believed possible. His systems pinged, letting him know something serious was broken inside somewhere. He looked up at the woman standing over him, her voice familiar.

He narrowed his eyes. "Hey, 'Neets. When did you get the extra eyes?"

She yanked him to his feet telekinetically. "I hate that name. I hated it the first time you uttered it."

Jack searched her face, seeing none of the woman he'd known in his ULTRA days. She'd been such an important part of their team back them. And now... "You've gone over to them. Why, Anita?"

"I'm to be your interrogator," she said, ignoring his question. "Will you answer my questions, or shall I rip the answers out of you telepathically?"

Jack straightened up as much as his throbbing body would allow. "Rip away, sweetheart. But this isn't over between us, Anita. You can count on it."

She chuckled quietly. "You don't know how little that scares me."

Her eyes glowed as she used her power to press in on Jack's mind, punching a hole in his natural psychic defenses. "Your shields have gotten stronger, Jack. I commend you." She pushed harder. "I have to be in further to find what I need."

Jack could feel the blood rushing through his veins, his heart pounding with adrenaline as he tried to fight the psychic attack. "You seem to have gotten more powerful yourself," he ground out between clenched teeth.

He thought of Rena's psychic touch and how different it was from Anita's. Rena's mind wrapped around you like a favorite blanket, easing hurt and taking care not to harm you. Anita was like a sledgehammer pounding on your skull. He watched her frown at him. Not once did she ask him any questions. From the look on her face when she first came in, he had a feeling the only thing she wanted to do was hurt him. And from the force of her psychic assault, she was achieving that very goal.

"You're thinking of a telepath named Rena," she murmured. "I know this girl. We have unfinished business."

He felt her pull back from his mind, and she released him from her telekinetic hold. His head throbbed from her psychic invasion. He crumpled to the floor, too hurt inside and out to even attempt standing. He barely heard what she said next.

"That was very informative, Jack," she sneered. "And when we've disposed of you, your girlfriend and that red-haired telepath are next. I look forward to our next session." She stooped next to his ear. "Of course, it might be fun to erase your memories and make you fall in love with me. Destroying you after that would be much more satisfying."

She stood and he listened to the clicking of her heels fade away. He pushed himself to his knees as he heard the agents closing in. Betrayed by a former teammate and knowing his friends wouldn't last much longer made the fight in him fade. Everyone important to him was going to die and for what? All because he wanted to be a hero.

A light, telepathic call soothed his mind. "*I'll stay with you until the end,*" Mindspell said.

****

Cap sliced through the door and Rena led the way to the stairwell door. She held her hand up, stopping the group. "Wait. Someone's trying to talk to me."

"*Rena, it's Mindspell. Have you come for Field Commander McClennan?*"

"Yes," Rena answered. "*And you, too. You need to come with us. The goon squad won't think twice about hurting you after we free him.*"

Mindspell paused. "*I'm in contact with him. He wants to die. He feels there's nothing left worth fighting for and that he's let everyone he loves down.*"

Rena felt her blood turn to ice. Jack couldn't give up. If he did, then there really was no hope at all. "*Keep him talking. We're almost there.*"

"*Will do, Rena.*"

Rena felt Mindspell withdraw and turned to the others. "We're officially out of time." She turned to Misty. "He needs you. Right now. Move it."

They charged down the steps, stopping to greet Mindspell at the third floor. They hurried down to the bottom and Cap nudged the door open a crack.

"I don't like this," he murmured to the small band with him. "Rena, scan the area."

"Five minds, one of them Jack's," she said. She swallowed hard several times to stop the nausea climbing in her throat. Anita's touch had left a nasty taint on his brain, making her stomach roil in protest. She detected the other telepath, but the connection was faint. She pushed harder and the link disappeared completely. "I picked up another telepath, but I can't find her anymore."

"If she shows or attacks, then we'll worry about her. Until then, we stay focused on getting Jack out of here."

Cap frowned as he checked the hallway beyond. "This seems too easy."

The small group stepped into the hallway and the door shut with a quiet click. Doors slid open on both sides of the hallway and agents stepped out, guns at the ready. Misty glared at them. They were all that stood between her and the man she loved. "I suggest you all get out of our way. If not, things are going to get real ugly, real quick."

In a single movement, they all fired. Captain Starblast jumped in front of Mindspell, his star shield absorbing the blasts. Misty turned desolid as Rena simply raised her telekinetic force field.

"Their psychic shields are way too powerful," she shouted to her teammates. "I can't punch through them, but I can sense Jack a little further down this hall."

Cap deflected a blast aimed at her. "Take Misty and get him. Mindspell and I will hold the door."

Rena and Misty set off down the hallway at a determined trot. She made a path through the human forest of agents. Forming a telekinetic bubble around herself, she flexed it, bouncing people out of her way while Misty stayed desolid so she couldn't be hurt.

Misty prayed Captain Starblast could hold out until

they got Jack and made it back to him and Mindspell. The agents seemed to be multiplying and who knew how badly Jack was hurt.

****

Misty was grateful for her power's side effect of disrupting electronics. The agents' armor shorted out whenever she walked through one of them.

Rena held her hand up and turned to her left. "He's in there."

Misty glared at the door. "Open the door, Rena. Please and thank you."

Rena redirected the force of her telekinesis and blew the door off the hinges. They hurried in and stopped short. Jack lay on his side, not moving, blood seeping out from under his head, his body battered and bruised. All of his gear was heaped in a far corner.

Misty looked at Jack, then raised her gaze to the agent. She started forward, her hands clenched into tight fists. Rena laid a hand on her shoulder. "This guy's mine. Don't bring yourself down to his level. Let me do it. Jack needs you now."

Misty ran to Jack's side and held him. Rena looked at him a few seconds longer, then walked to the agent who had blood dripping from his fist, stopping a few feet from him.

"This is the man my friend here loves. And, you know, I promised her I'd never hurt anyone again. I'd changed, I'd told her, and that life was all behind me," Rena said. She glanced at Misty, who looked up at her and nodded.

The agent took two steps toward her. "You haven't got it in you," he sneered. "Heroes don't have the stomach to do what's necessary."

194

Rena raised her hands pulling her telekinesis around her. "There's just one thing," she said. She flung out the force she'd built up, slamming the squad leader against the far wall and caving in his chest. "I didn't start out as a hero."

She dropped next to Misty. "How is he?"

Misty shook her head, feeling hot tears running down her face. "Not good. I can't wake him up. Rena, can you do something?"

She nodded, then knelt beside him. "Jack, it's Rena. Can you hear me?"

She scanned his mind, sighing in relief. "He's still in there, just out cold. Jack," she called again and added a telepathic echo to try and jar him awake. "It's time to get up because we're so not carrying you."

He groaned and his eyes fluttered open. "Misty? Rena? What are you doing here?"

She grinned. "We're rescuing you, silly boy. Even heroes need to be rescued once and awhile." She pulled him to his feet. "Misty, help me get him up. Can you help us any?"

"I'm surprised I can open my eyes," he moaned.

Misty pulled his arm over her shoulders. "Help us as much as you can, all right?"

He coughed and spit blood on the floor. "I'm not promising anything."

"Good enough." Rena turned to Misty. "I'm going to grab his stuff. I'm surprised they left it in here with him. He's going to need it when he's done using us as a crutch."

They walked to the door and Rena sent a mental message to Captain Starblast. *"We're coming out. We'll move as fast as we can."*

"I'll be watching for you," came his reply.

****

Mindspell watched Rena and Misty fight their way down to them. Jack was practically being carried by the two of them. As they got closer, she could see the strain on their faces. "They're not going to make," she yelled.

Cap turned to the trio coming down the hallway. "Hold the doorway. I'll get them."

"Go!" Mindspell yelled. She erected a telekinetic bubble, effectively stopping the agents from getting through. As soon as she had it up, it began to shrink. "I can't hold it, Cap. I'm not strong enough."

The captain was beside them in seconds. "I'll take him. Get us a path."

"I'm on it." She glanced at Mindspell. "Mindspell's shield is faltering. She can't hold it."

Rena telekinetically blew agents away from the door as they approached. Misty yanked the door open and the small team headed up the stairwell. Rena used a bit more power and twisted the door handle so it couldn't be opened without a whole lot of effort. "That'll show them who's boss."

Chapter Twenty-Six

Misty held Jack close with his head on her chest as Cap drove them to Challengers Headquarters. Rena had been tense all the way back to the car, her face grim every time Jack stopped to throw up blood. She sat in the front seat with the captain and stared out the window, Mindspell next to her.

Jack groaned and Misty held him tighter. "Oh, Jack. We all keep forgetting you're as human as the rest of us," she whispered. He sagged in her arms and blood dribbled from the corner of his mouth. "Don't give up on me now. Please."

Rena glanced over her shoulder. "He'd better not, or I'll kill him."

The captain screeched to a halt in front of his building where a member of his team had brought Jack's van. They were met by two of the Challengers and their medic, Stopwatch, who stopped time around Jack, thereby preventing him from getting worse. A four-armed man picked Jack up and carried him quickly to their medical ward.

Stopwatch turned to them. "As soon as I know anything, I'll tell you."

Misty crumpled into a chair, and Rena sat next to her, draping her arm around her shoulders. "Don't worry. He's tougher than you think. He'll be fine."

Misty turned tear-filled eyes to her. "How can you

be so sure?"

Rena winked at her. "Because anything else would put him on my bad side, and I don't think he wants to go there."

Misty smiled and sat back, letting her friend comfort her.

****

Jack opened his eyes as the room darkened. He frowned. Wasn't it dark when they went for Misty? How much time had gone by? He vaguely remembered Rena talking to him, helping him to escape. His mind felt fuzzy as he pushed to remember who else had been there. He turned his head and saw Misty sitting next to him. "Where am I?"

"Challengers Headquarters." She smiled and stroked his forehead. "How're you feeling?"

"Horrible." He swallowed, trying to loosen his throat to say something that sounded coherent. "But I'm alive, so I guess that's okay." He paused and stared at her. "How long was I there?"

She smoothed his hair back. "Only for a couple of hours. You've been sleeping for about twenty-four hours. Stopwatch said it was the sedatives, which she had to increase to make sure you rested enough to let your natural healing factor take over."

"Did you and Rena come back for me?"

She nodded. "Yes."

His head sank into the pillow. "It was too much too risk for just one person. Why would you endanger yourself like that?"

She kissed his forehead. "You would've done it for just one person, Jack. You know you would." She paused. "I did it because I love you." She smiled at him.

"I also did it because Rena helped me come up with a plan to get you out."

He frowned. "Are you sure? I can't picture Rena putting you and herself in danger just for me. I didn't think she liked me."

"You'd know if she didn't," Misty said. "She does keep insisting I give you the boot and marry an accountant."

"She would," Jack mumbled. "Was someone else with the two of you? I think there was, but I'm not sure."

Misty hesitated. "Cap went in with us. He's been trying to clear you ever since you were sent to prison. If you're up to it he wants to talk to you."

Jack remained silent. He'd accused his former friend of betrayal. He'd threatened to kill him, and still the captain stood by him. He felt sick and it had nothing to do with his current round of injuries. "Not tonight. I can't face him, tonight."

Misty stood. "I'll let you get some rest," she said.

He reached out and took her hand. "You said you love me."

She nodded.

"Know that I love you, too," he murmured. He tugged on her hand and she willingly sat on the bed. He reached up and pulled her face down to his, his breath warming her face as he cupped her cheek. "I have for a long time."

Misty leaned into his kiss, opening her lips against his, promising him, with her mouth, she's never let anyone hurt him again.

****

Jack stared at the ceiling. He thought about Misty

and Rena bringing Captain Starblast to get him. He would've laughed if he didn't know it to be true. In his early days at ULTRA, he was always glad to work with the captain and the Challengers. They were his favorite team. They were also the favorite team of everyone in the city. Every member was popular and there was always new graffiti to proclaim how much the heroes were loved.

When he was first arrested, there was only one person in his mind to call and that was Captain Starblast. He frowned at the memory invading his mind.

When he'd been taken to the visitor's room, he'd been so sure everything was going to turn out all right. It had been all he could do not to taunt the guards that he'd been wrongly accused. Then he'd seen the contents of the envelope. He'd pleaded with Captain Starblast to believe him and not the papers laying on the table. When the captain had said he had to turn over to the authorities, his temper had flared out of control. He'd accused the captain of being bought before threatening to kill him

Those words were the last he'd ever spoken to the city's most popular hero. Jack looked around the room. Now, not only was he in Captain Starblast's building, the hero had brought him here.

From what he'd just learned from Misty, the captain really hadn't betrayed him and had always been on his side. The man had been as manipulated as he'd been, and somehow the news didn't cheer him at all.

****

Misty closed the door to the room in the Challengers living quarters on the floor above the hospital wing. It was spacious and had reminded her of a luxury hotel room when she'd first seen it. It was decorated in pale blue and had a private bathroom. She smiled broadly and twirled around the room, finally collapsing on the bed.

"He loves me," she whispered. "Rena said he did." Misty thought Rena knew Jack better than anyone. "It better be because she's a telepath."

The door opened. "Of course it's because I'm a telepath," Rena said as she came in. "He's got too much baggage and a red-headed marriage is just asking for trouble. He's all yours." She jumped on the bed next to Misty. "I take it the big oaf finally admitted he loves you?"

"Yes, he did, and stop calling him an oaf."

Rena winked at her. "No, I don't see that happening. How's he doing?"

Misty shrugged. "He says he feels horrible but alive. Stopwatch said he has a healing factor that's off the charts, so he should be back on his feet sooner than we originally thought. I get the feeling he's been hurt more often than he lets on."

Rena laughed. "You think? The army, Interpol, ULTRA, then surgery, and being on the run. I'd say he's an old hand at the injury game."

"I don't want him to get hurt anymore."

"You can't restrain him, you know."

Misty gave her a small smile. "I know. But what if he really doesn't want me when he gets better? What if it was just the medicine talking?"

She stood, giving an exaggerated sigh. "That's it. I'm done. I am *so* not doing this tonight. I swear I'm going to need therapy for the rest of my life. So, before I go completely nuts, I'm going back to the mansion.

Tell Jack I'll see you guys in the morning. I have a meeting with Michael Frailer."

"What for?"

"Just got to update ULTRA's lord high mucky muck on what's been going on. Good night."

Misty got ready for bed and crawled in between the sheets. The man of her dreams, her Mr. Right, loved her. If she had played it careful, the way Rena told her when she first met Jack, she never would've found love.

Chapter Twenty-Seven

Jack opened his eyes as the bright, warm, summer sunlight streamed into the room. He blinked several times, trying to remember where he'd been taken. There was no strong antiseptic smell, no voices drifting in from the hallway, so it wasn't a hospital. He thought a minute longer. Challengers HQ. He never thought he'd see the inside of that place again.

He tried to rise and unhook all the monitors as the door opened. He frowned at the man who entered, and his chest went cold. Jack's hand curled around a weapon that wasn't there.

"Don't get up," Cap said. "You need to give yourself more time to heal."

Jack lay back. "Misty told me some interesting things last night," he said, turning an expressionless face to the captain. The hero wore no micro chainmail armor this morning, just sweat pants and a T-shirt.

The captain stood to the side and allowed a short girl with sparkling white hair to come in, carrying a food tray. "Stopwatch wasn't sure you could handle solid food after your internal injuries, but she changed her mind after she ran your tests this morning. Your healing factor is as close to natural regeneration as I've ever seen. Eat first. Your questions have waited this long. A few more minutes won't hurt."

Jack watched her put the tray down and helped him

sit a little higher. She made sure he had everything before leaving the room.

He looked at Cap. "New member?"

"Got to put new blood in the ranks. Some of us are feeling the effects of too many battles."

Jack ate in silence as Cap leaned against the wall. Questions burned in him as he watched the hero out of the corner of his eye. He'd waited for this day, but he'd seen it going a little differently. He had no weapons, no armor, and was laid up after having the hell kicked out of him.

He finished and pushed the table away, turning to stare at the man across the room. "Misty said you've been working for years on my behalf. Is this true?"

The hero nodded. "The last time we spoke, when you saw the evidence I found, I couldn't shake the feeling something wasn't right. I decided to do some checking. The results were...interesting."

Jack's body tensed. "You found something that could've supported what I was saying and you kept quiet? Why didn't you at least tell me?"

The captain moved to sit in the chair next to the bed. "I wanted to but didn't want to get your hopes up. Soon after that, you disappeared."

"How do I know you're telling me the truth?" Jack looked over at him, and his eyes narrowed. "We didn't have a good last meeting."

Cap leaned forward. "I understand you don't trust me, and that's fine. It's going to take time." He stood and paced. "I called Michael Frailer. I don't think you've had a chance to meet him. He's the current ULTRA commander. He's coming by to talk to you today."

Jack's hand twitched as he wished for any kind of weapon as he frowned at Cap.

The hero simply smiled. "He just wants to talk to you. No agents, no warrants, nothing for you to worry about. You're currently under my protection, on my personal word to the commander. You apparently have two guardian Angels looking out for you."

Jack frowned. Misty he could understand, but Rena…? "Are you sure?"

"Positive." Cap stood next to him. "Michael also wants to know exactly what you learned thirteen years ago, and how George Fenmore is involved."

"How does he know all this?" Jack asked.

The captain chuckled. "Rena and Misty have explained about everything the two of them had uncovered."

Jack was really confused, now. He looked up at the captain. He opened his mouth, but Cap held up a hand, stopping him.

"I'm not sure of the particulars," the hero said, "but Misty is still here and will be in to see you when we're done. A couple of friends of yours showed up last night, also."

The only sound for several long moments was the steady beeping of the monitors hooked to Jack saying he was recovering just fine. Jack thought about what he'd been told and frowned as he ended up with more questions now than before.

Captain Starblast stood at the end of his bed. "So are you still planning my immediate demise or can I stop worrying?"

Jack's gaze shot to him and he relaxed, seeing the grin on the hero's face. "Keep worrying for now. I'll let you know if I change my mind."

Starblast nodded. "Fair enough."

Misty walked in, nodding to Cap as he left, heading straight to Jack's bed. "Good morning. You're looking better."

Jack gave her a skeptical glance. "I just need to rest and let all the beautiful nurses come and take care of me." He took her hand, pressing a small kiss to the back of it. "You wouldn't want me to get up too soon and have a relapse, would you?"

She grinned and shook her head. "I knew it. You're a typical male who needs to be babied constantly."

He pulled her down next to him. "Only if you're volunteering."

"Pick me," she whispered just before kissing him lightly.

"Hey, you two, break it up," Frank said from the doorway. He led Amy into the room and let her sit in the chair by the bed. He made sure she was comfortable and didn't need anything before turning to Jack, who watched him with open amusement.

Amy grinned. "I keep telling him I'm not made of glass. I'm fine. I've been fine, but he won't leave me alone."

"I just want to make sure she doesn't overtire herself," Frank said, sounding a little more than slightly defensive.

"How did you guys find me?" Jack asked, deciding to ignore Frank's adoring looks at Amy and Amy's pink cheeks every time he did.

"Rena telepathically called me," Amy said. "She said she thought you'd feel better if we were here with you."

Jack glanced at Misty. "Did you know about this?" he asked her.

Misty shook her head. "Rena really does care, Jack. For all her quirks, she knows what people need."

"I just can't believe she would do this for me," Jack said, his voice low. "I mean, she made no secret of her dislike for me."

"I think it was more because she thought you hurt me," Misty said. "She's kind of over-protective."

Jack just nodded and took Amy's hand. "This means the world to us."

"I'll let you guys have some time and check on you later." Misty kissed him again and left.

Jack watched her leave then turned to his friends. They'd been so close and now, things were going to get ugly for the whole team. He wanted to tell them everything would work out the way they wanted, but he was sick of lies.

"How are things progressing?"

Frank shook his head. "Not good. No one on the street is talking." He paused. "Everyone's gone."

Jack trembled, a deep, internal chill pushing its way out to his skin. "What about Mexico? Is he safe?"

Amy smiled. "He's safe. The more people stopped talking, the more he knew something was wrong. He's at the country house." She wrinkled her nose. "And I told him to burn those rags he wears. They reek."

Jack grinned, knowing Mexico would probably have argued, but eventually would've done it. Nobody told Amy no. He looked up. "Frank, I need you to find Cyber-X."

Frank's eyes opened wide. "Are you sure? Wasn't he trying to bring you in recently?"

"Yes, but we've established a sort of truce, and we need help." Jack turned to Amy. "My girl, you've got the harder job."

She sat forward. "What? I'll do anything to help."

Jack squeezed her hand. "The head of ULTRA is coming by today to talk to me. I want you to talk to him, too. You know more about the paper trail than any of us."

Frank began to pace. "Are you sure about this guy? How do you know you can trust him?"

"Rena requested Michael not do anything until he had the full story. As a telepath, she'd have known if he couldn't be trusted. I think we have more allies in this than we first believed."

"Ha! I told you so," Frank said, grinning wide when Jack just scowled at him.

"Jack?" Amy asked quietly. "What happens to you now?"

He had thought long and hard about what would happen to him, and he had no illusions about his fate. "I'm probably looking at life in the HighPower Containment Facility or possible execution."

Amy choked back a small sob. "After all you've done to protect them? They wouldn't."

"They would," he said quietly. "I don't know what Commander Frailer's going to say when he hears our story, but we've got to face the fact I'm not a free man anymore."

Amy kissed his cheek. "We know, but it doesn't make it hurt any less." She stood back, taking Frank's hand. "We'll let you get some rest. See you later."

He lay back, letting the silence enfold him. The day he'd been waiting for had finally arrived and he had nothing. All he had was his word and that hadn't been trusted for years. Would the ULTRA commander believe him? Jack closed his eyes and prayed the answer was yes.

Chapter Twenty-Eight

Rena arrived in the late morning with a bag of clothes for Misty. The two sat in the Challengers' kitchen, sipping orange juice.

Misty ran her hand down the side of the glass. "Frank and Amy are with him." She glanced at Rena. "That was really decent of you to call them."

The red-head grinned. "Yeah, I know. I figured better to have them here than have Jack trying to run off to contact them."

Misty punched her lightly on the arm. "You did it because you're a nice person."

"I'm going to ignore that," Rena said. "Speaking of Jack, how's our little patient this morning?"

"He looks a hundred percent better than last night. He should be back on his feet soon and back in action by the end of next week."

Rena whistled. "That's a serious healing factor."

They clinked glasses, toasting Jack's returning health. Misty looked at her friend. "Jack's confused about why you went through so much to get him back. I mean, I love him. I'm supposed to do things like that, not you."

"Good," Rena said. "A little uncertainty is good for him."

Misty shook her head. "I think he might be wanting you now instead of me."

Rena narrowed her eyes as she glanced at Misty. "You'd better be kidding. I already told you, I don't want him."

Misty shrugged. "He keeps talking about you. How do I know he isn't having second thoughts about me and our relationship?"

"How about the fact that I was the middle man while you guys weren't speaking?" Rena drummed her fingers on the table. "You know, I'm ready to strangle both of you. He loves you. You love him. Why can't the two of you leave me out of it?"

Misty stood. "I'm going to check in with Cap. You coming?"

"No. I've got something else that needs to be seen to."

Rena marched down to Jack's room and flung open the door. "I really don't need this," she said, trying hard not to shout. "What exactly is your problem?"

Jack watched Rena stomp over to him. "What do you want? I swear I've seen more of you than I have of Misty, lately."

Rena leaned close and scowled. "And whose fault is that? Do something to reassure Misty, or I swear, I'll knock some more sense in there. Is that what you want?"

Jack frowned back at her. "You're the telepath, you tell me."

"No," she bit out. "It'd be like reading a children's book." She stepped back and folded her arms. "Misty thinks you're getting the hots for me. You're the only one who can set her straight." She paused and stared at him. *"So set her straight!"*

The two of them stared at each for several seconds

before Jack looked away. "She can't believe I'd give her up for you. No offense."

Rena grinned. "None taken. I'd kill you before the week was out. I know what you want to tell her. Let me get her for you. This needs to be done right now." She patted his arm. "No more waiting, Jack. No more hesitation. Don't lose her because you wanted to wait for the perfect moment."

Jack nodded. "You aren't influencing me, are you?"

Rena gave him a horrified look. "Me? Do something like that? You must have me confused with an unethical telepath." She headed for the door, turned, and winked at him. "I'll get Misty."

****

Jack stared at the ceiling while he waited for Misty. Did Rena plant a suggestion in his mind to make him do this now? Unless she decided to tell him, he'd probably never know.

"Rena said you needed to see me." She hurried to his bed. "Are you in pain? What can I do?"

Jack clutched her hand and knew, whether the telepath influenced him or not, she was right. "Red pushed me into doing this now. She said no more waiting. I wanted to see how things were going to play out, but she's right. I have something to say and it needs to be said now."

Misty sat on his bed, waiting for him to continue. "What?"

"Misty, I've loved you since I first saw you," he said. "Please don't doubt that." He took a deep breath. "Would you do me the honor of becoming my wife?"

Misty blinked and stared at him. "You want to

212

marry me?"

He nodded. "You know what you're getting. I'm a criminal, a mercenary, a cybernetic renegade, and I'm probably going to be in prison for the rest of my life. All I know is how much I love you, how much I need you."

He watched tears slip down her cheeks as she stared at him. "You're all I've wanted since the day we met," she said. "So, yes, ex-Field Commander Jack McClennan, I'll marry you, and whatever the future holds, we'll face it together."

He pulled her closer, and he ran his hand behind her neck then pulled her face to his. "Good," he murmured against her lips. "As long as I have you, I can face anything."

Misty ran her hands over his chest and deepened the kiss they shared. She sighed when she felt his hand move up under her shirt, warming her bare skin. His touch climbed higher, skimming the bottom of her breast when the door opened.

Rena walked in, and Jack recognized the man with her as ULTRA Commander Michael Frailer. He had seen pictures of him in the newspaper when he'd been installed as the new head of ULTRA. He'd also watched the ceremony on television.

"Can you believe these two?" Rena said from the doorway. She winked at ULTRA's commander, Michael Frailer. "Push them into getting together, and they're all over each other."

Misty jumped off the bed and glared at her friend. "You did that on purpose, Red."

Rena just chuckled. "Paybacks are a bitch, my friend. And I still owe you a couple."

"Ouch."

"I'd like to hear the whole story on that one. But another day," Michael said to Jack, then turned to the two Angels. "If you'll excuse us?"

"Sure thing," Rena said. "Later, Jack." She pushed Misty through the doorway.

****

"I'm Michael Frailer, the current head of ULTRA," he said, sticking out his hand. "Everyone just calls me Mike." He grinned. "Or boss. And you're the infamous Jack McClennan."

Jack shook his hand reluctantly. "That's me." He gestured to the bed. "Not a very impressive first meeting, is it?"

Mike smiled and pulled papers out of his briefcase, arranging them on the bedside table. "A lot of agents still talk about you and your team, about how good you were. I don't think the setting matters." He glanced at a file. "Your ULTRA record has never been equaled."

"Thanks," Jack mumbled.

Mike glanced at him. "Relax. There's more to this case than what appears on the surface. Hopefully, we'll get everything sorted out the way it should be." He shuffled some papers into a different order. "Now, it says you insisted that a hidden group was behind everything you were accused of. Care to elaborate?"

Jack closed his eyes. "George Fenmore, Donald Harrington, and their entire teams. Anita Haines. She was my team telepath but now she works for them. I killed most of the team members when I escaped the hospital."

Mike made several notes while Jack talked, but stopped and looked up at him. "You're admitting to murder?"

"Unless I'm honest with you, you'll have no reason to trust me." He pushed himself up higher in the bed. "I tried to get as many as I could when I broke out. I stole my ULTRA armor and assembled my team."

Mike shook his head. "And I put Fenmore in charge of the panel to find you," he muttered. "No wonder you didn't want to come to me. I'm so sorry."

Jack nodded, not trusting himself to say anything. That the commander would apologize, told him volumes about the man's character.

"Do you know what happened to your original evidence?" Mike asked.

"I was told they kept it to remind themselves not to slip up again." He glanced at Mike. "That's all my team and I were to them—a slip up—a mistake that needed to be corrected."

"Can you give me the names of your team members?" Mike asked as he pulled a fresh sheet of paper out from the bottom of the stack.

Jack nodded. He didn't want to, but Mike would need to talk to them to corroborate his story. "My network has grown over the years. My two main agents are here. I'd like to shield them, but I can't, can I?'

Mike shook his head. "I'm sorry. I'll involve them as little as possible. To stay with you this long, to go through what they have, I'll not ask them to break their loyalty or their promises to you."

"Good enough," Jack said. "Everything did, they did because I asked them to. They were acting under direct orders from their field commander. That should be taken into consideration."

Mike smiled. "There's a lot to be taken into

consideration."

"A young girl, a telepath, came with us when Rena came for me," Jack said. "Her name's Mindspell, and she's from HelixCorp."

"She's with us for training," Mike said, jotting down more notes. "HelixCorp didn't have the right people to properly train her."

"Fenmore was using her as a tracker to find me."

Mike frowned. "She wasn't supposed to leave the building. She could barely use her powers. Fenmore is going to have a lot more to answer for than I first thought when I find him."

Jack nodded. He was beginning to warm to the ULTRA commander as much as he tried not to. Michael Frailer seemed to be just the person he needed. He looked up. "I'm surprised at myself for wanting to trust you. It's been so long since I talked to anyone in authority." He smiled a little.

"You were one of ULTRA's best." Mike asked, "Do you miss it?"

Jack nodded. "Almost every day. After this mess started, heroes I worked with, heroes I knew, turned their backs on me. All I heard was 'I never expected *him* to turn traitor.' And 'he seemed like such a good person.' It turned out the hero population actually had no use for me. So I returned their contempt."

Mike chuckled quietly. "When we get this straightened out, there're going to be a lot of heroes with some pretty red faces." His eyes took on a faraway look.

Jack watched for a few minutes. "What are you thinking about?"

"I was a squad leader when your case broke," Mike

said. "Things just didn't seem to fit. I wondered why you sent Captain Starblast for evidence if it was so incriminating. I asked around and did some investigating on my own, but nobody would talk to me. I was getting ready to come see you at the prison, when I immediately was shipped out on remote tour. Spent almost two years in that hell hole."

Jack shook his head. "I guess I did have people on my side after all. It didn't seem like it at the time, so I became what everyone said I was; a cold, heartless, killing machine."

Mike rose and clapped him on the shoulder. "We'll talk again. I'd like to speak with your friends briefly before I go." He smiled. "I believe in your innocence fully. Convincing me was the hard part. It'll be all downhill from here."

Jack wasn't so sure.

Chapter Twenty-Nine

Misty turned as Mike walked into the briefing room. This was it. She wanted to hear what he thought but, at the same time, dreaded what he would say. Her future with Jack was in Mike's hands and his opinion was important to them. A large knot formed in the pit of her stomach and she wished he hadn't eaten anything that morning.

"So, what do you think of our guest?" Cap asked.

Mike laid his briefcase on the table and sat. "I believe he's innocent of the original crimes, but then, I always did. He's admitted to some new ones, so as much as I don't like it, I have to acknowledge them."

Misty glanced toward the door. She wanted to run down to Jack's room and help him escape again but knew that wouldn't be smart. "Are you sure? Is there anything you can do for him?"

"Don't worry. I have a few ideas I need to discuss with other people."

"I can't help worrying," she mumbled, her voice shaking.

He patted her shoulder. "Everything should go the way I hope."

Mike shuffled through his papers and pulled out the one he wanted. "I need to see Frank DiNello and Amy Rogers. Are they both still here?"

Cap nodded. "Yes. I've invoked the Hero

Sanctuary Law. If any more of Jack's team come in, they'll all be protected here."

Mike nodded. "I know you'll do your best to help Jack's team. I don't think I would expect you to do anything less for him." He turned to Rena. "You brought a young girl here named Mindspell. Is she still here?"

Rena nodded. "Yes. After we rescued Jack, I didn't think it was safe to leave her at ULTRA. She'll be with me until this is wrapped up."

"I'm going to have to talk to her," Mike said, making more notes.

Rena chewed her lip and nodded. "She's not going back to HelixCorp."

Mike narrowed his eyes as he looked at the telepath. "Any reason?"

"More than you think."

Mike stared at Rena a minute longer, made a notation, and turned to the rest. "Well, let's get the ball rolling. Cap, if you'd be so kind as to show me where people are, I'll get the initial interviews out of the way. Then, I'll know how to proceed."

Misty stood and shook Mike's hand. "Thank you for listening. I'm glad I was right about you wanting to help him."

"I'll do everything I can to make this as easy as possible for him and for you." He smiled. "It's all about the paperwork now."

****

Misty hurried down to Jack's room and opened the door quietly, only to find him sitting up and yanking wires and patches off his body. She shook her head.

"You shouldn't do that, you know," she said.

"I'm sick of lying in bed," he said, not stopping until the last wire lay on the floor. "Besides, I feel better."

Misty folded her arms, giving him a stern look. "You've had internal injuries."

He stood on wobbly legs. "So, what's your point?"

She hurried over to him and slipped his arm around her shoulders while he steadied himself. "My point, Mr. Macho, is that even indestructible cyborgs need to heal. I don't want you ending up destructible because you're too stubborn to listen."

He took a few steps. "This junk I'm carrying around is older, experimental systems. They need to be kept active or they seize."

She sighed dramatically. "I suppose since you have rapid healing, you'll be all right." She helped him walk around the room a couple of times. "A couple of days ago, you were throwing up blood and now you're walking."

He winked. "I'm full of surprises."

She let her gaze roam over his body. "I know. I love your surprises."

He held her tighter, not wanting to let her go. "Maybe later, I'll give you another one." He straightened up. "Right now, though, I need a shower and pants."

Misty ran her hand over his chest. "How about a sponge bath and I'll consider the pants?"

He lightly traced an X over her heart, smiling when she shivered. "Promise?"

"Anything you want to hear," she whispered.

He smiled. "Right now, I think I need a practical shower."

She elbowed his ribs. "Killjoy."

Thirty minutes later, Jack came out, rubbing his hair and wearing a pair of Cap's sweat pants. Misty watched him pull his hair back and decided watching him was better than anything on TV.

"Stopwatch wants you back in the medical ward until she checks you out," Misty said. "She just wants to make sure there're no complications."

Jack nodded. "Tonight, I want to be with you."

"You will," Misty said.

They opened the door to Jack's room, and Rena was stretched out on the bed. "Greetings, fellow heroes," she said.

"Must you always make yourself at home on my furniture?" Jack asked.

Rena swung her legs over the side of the bed and stood. "Technically, this really isn't your bed, so I'm allowed."

Misty rolled her eyes. "Rena, don't aggravate the man."

The red-head shrugged. "I'm so unloved." She walked over to the couple and tossed a small package at Jack. "Here. I got what you wanted and I don't even get a thank you."

She was almost out the door when Jack grabbed her and kissed her. "Thanks." He turned to Misty. "Surprising the resident telepath? Priceless."

Misty burst out laughing. Rena's face said it all.

Rena punched Jack on the arm. "You're welcome. Just remember what I said earlier. Paybacks are a bitch."

They watched Rena leave, and Jack couldn't wait to see Misty's expression when she learned what he asked Rena to pick up.

He led her over to his bed and they sat. Jack took a deep breath.

He turned to Misty, surprised to see his hands shaking a little. Nerves? No, it had to be from moving around. He took another deep breath and opened the box.

"Misty, I know I've already asked you, but will you marry me?"

Misty looked at the ring in the small black box and Jack held his breath waiting. He thought it fit her temperament and personality better than the traditional sort of ring. This was the shape of a flower with diamonds for petals and emeralds for leaves, with a blue star sapphire in the center.

She gazed up at Jack, tears in her eyes. "I'll say it a million times if you like," she whispered. "I'll marry you wherever and whenever you want."

She threw her arms around his neck, kissing him with a slow simmering passion that steadily rose. She sighed when his arms pulled her closer, and they fell back on the bed. Jack pulled Misty on top of him, groaning softly when she straddled him. She leaned forward, her breasts gently brushing his chest, and he slid his hands up to caress her skin under her shirt.

"I've missed the feel of you too much recently," he whispered.

She ran her finger down his cheek. "I missed you, too. We have right now, you know. I think people will leave us alone for a few minutes."

Jack smiled at her. "Are you sure? It could be embarrassing."

She pressed herself closer to him, smiling when she

felt his immediate reaction. "Let's get embarrassed."

She eased his pants down his legs then stood, marveling at the sight of him. She ran a hand across his thigh, just stopping from the heart of him. She moved her hand up across his stomach, deliberately ignoring the part throbbing for her touch.

"You're going to drive me crazy," he gasped as she pressed light kisses across his midsection.

Misty looked up at him. "I know."

She moved away and slowly peeled off her clothes, giving him a coy smile as he watched her, and then she held her hand out and went willingly when he tugged her down next to him.

"My turn," he whispered before claiming her right breast with his mouth. As his hand moved closer to the part of her his touch missed so much, he nudged her thighs apart, and she opened them, giving him all the access he wanted.

She dug her fingers into his hair, and he skimmed over her sensitive center before rubbing her gently. Her breath came out in short gasps. And her hands moved to his shoulders, tightly clinging to him. Then he covered her mouth with his, capturing her cry as her passion took her flying.

He knelt between her legs, smiling as his gaze roamed over her. Her body still quivered, and he touched her one more time, smiling as she melted into his touch.

"I've missed touching you," he murmured. He made himself slowly enter her, savoring the feel of her wrapped around him. "And I've really missed feeling you around me."

Misty grinned at him. "You'll never be without me

again. You know that, right?"

He filled her completely and kissed her. "I know."
****

Stopwatch checked his natural eye and nodded, making a notation on his medical chart. She ran a scanner over his cybernetic parts and pronounced no damage. She looked at his vital signs and frowned.

"Your heart rate's up, and so is your temperature and blood pressure. Any problems?"

Jack winked at Misty. "I feel fine."

Stopwatch turned and looked at Misty standing off to the side. "Are your vitals up, too?"

Misty just smiled and looked around the room.

"If you can do what I think you've just done, I feel comfortable letting you move to Misty's room." She pointed at him with the pencil. "Don't overdo it for a few days."

Jack winked. "You got it, doc."

Stopwatch just smiled and shook her head. "We've got minors here. Just be discreet."

Jack gave her a hurt look. "I'm the very soul of discretion."

Misty choked out a laugh, trying to maintain a respectful silence. Finally unable to contain it, she just gave in. "Yeah, right, discretion."

Jack frowned at Misty when Stopwatch walked over to her. "That means you too, Miss Angel."

Misty opened her eyes wide. "You mean I can't jump him in the hallway?"

Stopwatch chuckled. "Get out of my medical ward. You're both taking up too much space."

Misty led Jack down to her room and shut the door behind them. "Okay. We made it here without corrupting any of the kids. What now?"

Jack pulled her into his arms. "Let's see how healed I really am."

"We just did," she murmured. "Are you sure you're up to it?"

He pulled her tightly against him, and she felt how much he was up to it. She nibbled his jaw as her hands worked their way inside the waistband of his pants. She smiled as she felt his muscles tense under her hands.

"I think we can handle another session."

They stripped out of their clothes, and Misty made Jack lay down on her bed. "Stopwatch said for you not to overdo it." She straddled him, slowly easing herself down. "This time, I'll do all the work."

****

Jack held her close, wishing everything was behind them and he wouldn't have to leave her. Rena's voice kept coming back to him, telling him to stop waiting and do something.

"I want us to get married as soon as possible," he said, pulling her tighter to him.

Misty sat up and gazed at him. "Why? You know something I don't?"

He traced her jaw. "No. I just want everything to be done before we go in to break the Council."

"A small wedding will upset my friends," she said, closing her eyes to revel in his touch.

"We'll have a big one when we win," he said. "For now, I just want to legalize everything."

He let his hand drift down to the valley between her breasts and then over them. He smiled when her body immediately responded to his touch. He let it go lower and watched her face.

"We'll win," she whispered. "Because now you owe me."

His hands roamed her body. "How about if I pay you back some of it right about now?" he asked.

Her arms went around his neck, and she pulled him closer until their lips were a breath apart. "Deal," she said before closing the tiny gap that separated them.

Chapter Thirty

Jack took Misty's hand while Cap led them to the workout room, where a priest stood talking to other members of the Challengers. The priest appeared to be in his mid-thirties, and his light brown hair was disheveled. Dust covered his clothes, and he had gauze wrapped around his left hand. A five o'clock shadow darkened his cheeks, but his green eyes were bright and kind.

"I contacted a local priest whose parish isn't far from here," Cap said. "He's going to perform your ceremony."

Jack looked suspiciously at the captain. "Does he know who we are?"

"He has many ties to the paranormal community. He can keep our secret safe."

Jack glanced at Misty then back at the priest. "He's the first one I've seen who needs a shave."

Cap grinned. "He's not a typical man of the cloth. He and his friend just finished banishing some low level demons and he hasn't had a chance to get cleaned up. He came as soon as I called him."

Misty stood beside Jack, Rena took her place to Misty's left, and Cap stood to Jack's right. The rest of the Challengers' team stood witnessing while the priest performed the brief ceremony.

As Misty kissed her new husband, she thought of

the future. Would they be able to have the large wedding they talked about? Or would her fears be realized? Would he be locked away from her forever? She held him a little tighter, smiling slightly when he squeezed her before stepping back. She gazed at his face, not used to seeing him without the eye-patch and not looking like an angry storm was about to be unleashed.

After completing the ceremony, Cap walked the priest to the door, and Rena turned to Misty. "So Jack's going to go through this again, except on a larger scale, when this is over?"

Misty turned to her. "Will you stop reading my thoughts?"

Rena shook her head. "Not until I'm sure he won't screw this up a second time."

"He won't." Misty turned to see her new husband walk to the control panel and program in a workout session. She blushed as she thought about their recent "workouts." She was ready for another one right then.

"Oh, please, stop," Rena said. "I do *not* need to know any of this."

Misty grinned. "Then stop peeking."

"Turn down the libido or I may not have any choice except to jump him myself," Rena said. "Remember, I've got a power glitch. And I can appreciate the man now."

Misty just smiled and walked away, leaving Rena to follow her. The two Angels turned at the door and watched Jack start a workout routine. Misty had appreciated him from the first day they'd met.

****

The next day, Jack rolled his shoulders as he faced

off with Cap and several other members of the
Challengers. He glanced behind him, noting the spot
where the strongman of the Challengers' team stood.
The girl who had brought him his breakfast when he
was still laid up stood behind Cap and to his left. A
buzzer sounded and Cap feinted to the right. Jack
followed him, not falling for the diversionary tactic.

"That's the oldest trick in the book, Cap," Jack
said, throwing up his arm to block the punch coming at
him. He dropped and took out the hero with a leg
sweep, rolling out of the grasp of the big guy. He came
up near the girl, barely ducking as she fired a sparkling
blast of violet energy.

The Challengers strongman charged up behind
him, grabbing him in a bone-crushing hug as he pinned
Jack's arms to his sides while lifting him off the floor.
Instead of struggling to free himself, he fired a small
missile from his gauntlet into the big man's foot. "It's a
good thing you're damn near indestructible. Otherwise,
I'd have had to do something a lot more painful," Jack
said.

The large man dropped him, and Cap's shield
clipped his breastplate to bounce up and glance off his
forehead. "Give up, my friend," Cap called.

Jack grabbed the shield, giving the captain a
wicked grin as he wiped at the blood starting to run
down his cheek. He tapped his head where the shield
cut him open. "Metal skull, Cap. Not going down."

Jack threw the shield, knowing Cap would duck
and counted on the girl's inexperience not to avoid
being hit. Cap dove at Jack, taking out his legs. Jack
rolled out of it, simultaneously pulling his sonic rifle. A
quick check to make sure it was on low power, and he

fired, stunning Cap, effectively taking him out of the fight.

He turned, hearing the lumbering man charge him from behind and fired his flash pistol, shutting down the attack. Jack jumped at him, hitting him with a head butt, knocking him over.

The buzzer sounded again as Captain Starblast shook off the effects of the sonic pulse to look up into a rifle, ending in Jack's grinning face.

"I think I'm ready now, Cap," Jack said, offering his old friend a hand up. He watched as the Challengers members got to their feet.

Cap nodded. "You didn't even break a sweat. We can go in any time now."

"Mike will be happy to hear that," Jack said. "He's anxious to get this whole thing wrapped up."

"Jack," Cap said quietly, holding his hand out. "It's good to have you back."

He stared at Captain Starblast before taking the hero's hand in a firm grip. "It's nice to be working with you again. I guess you can stop looking over your shoulder."

Cap grinned. "Thanks." He nodded at the control room. "I think someone was watching you."

Jack turned and saw Misty standing there. He waved to her, smiling as she waved back.

****

The next afternoon, Misty looked up as Frailer entered the briefing room. "I need to ask you something before the others get here."

Frailer began laying folders in front of the chairs that would soon be occupied. "Ask away. I'll try to answer anything I can."

She stopped, not wanting to ask the question, but needing to know. "What's going to happen to him when this is over?"

The commander turned to her. "You're talking about a complicated case. Let's say we get the original evidence back and everything goes as planned. I know I can clear Jack of the original charges."

He glanced at her. "After that, it's a crap shoot. It depends on what the evidence shows, and what can be proven. He's committed some serious crimes, even if it was for the greater good."

Misty sank down in a chair, her legs refusing to hold her up any longer. "You're still going to help him, right?"

Frailer smiled and nodded. "Of course. I've got a plan in place that I'm discussing with people more powerful than I am. Let's just take it one day at a time."

She sat back and folded her arms, trying to work off an internal chill. Mike seemed confident that everything would work out fine, but would it? She'd feel better if he would just tell her what he had in mind. Things had a way of going in unexpected directions in the hero business, and with this whole ugly situation, it just might take that left turn at Albuquerque.

Jack walked in the room with Cap leading in his team. Misty's heart leapt at the sight on him, and she refused to allow despair to rule whatever time they had together. She smiled as he took his place next to her

"We can go whenever you want," Jack said.

"Excellent!" Mike said breaking out in a broad smile. "This time, we'll have the proper ending to this situation."

"I hope you're right," Jack murmured. "If we blow

it, we'll never ferret them out."

Rena walked in and looked at the assembled heroes. "Let's see. We have the ULTRA commander, the team leader of the Challengers, and the infamous Jack McClennan. Talk about too many chiefs." She grinned. "So who's running this little shindig?"

They all looked at Jack. "I guess it's me for right now."

"I don't see Frank and Amy. Where'd they run off to?"

Jack glanced at her. "They're on special assignments for me. I'll fill them in when they get back." He turned to Mike. "I'm still in contact with my old team. If you want them, I can get them."

Mike nodded. "If the Grave Diggers squad knew this was going down and they weren't in on it, they'd kill me. Bring them on board."

Jack smiled. Mike appeared to know his team as well as he did. "I'll get the word out."

"Now, on to the matter at hand." Mike turned on the projector and showed the floor plans. He pointed to the fifth floor. "This is where the stairs ended, correct?" The heroes nodded. "Then if there's more to this area, there must a concealed entrance somewhere. Jack, any ideas?"

Jack stood, studying the diagram. "Probably here," he said, pointing to the east wall. "It would go right under the main building, and they wouldn't have had to do much to set it up. Extend the wiring and piping, and it's ready. The regular ULTRA wouldn't even notice it." He glanced at Mike. "Sorry."

"It's all right. I agree with you," Mike said. "What do you think will be the most effective way to attack?"

"I've been giving that some thought," he said. "I think two teams. Descend the stairs about five minutes apart. That way, no team is on their own too long. Mike, I'd like you to take a team of trustworthy agents and secure the perimeter around the building. If any agents get by us, you can stop them." Jack nodded to Rena. "When we've finished, I'll have Rena telepathically call you to come in for the final sweep."

Mike stood, staring at the screen. "You know who you want on your teams, yet?"

Jack nodded. "I'll take Rena, Frank, and the Challengers' new girl with me. I'd like Captain Starblast to take Misty, Mindspell, and the Challengers' muscle. We'll each have a telepath so we won't need radios."

"Sounds like a good plan," Mike said, gathering his papers. "I've already started selecting agents. Let's set it for two days, then."

Jack nodded as he shook Mike's hand. "I may have another person coming with us. He's trustworthy, and we can use him. Keep in touch."

"You too," Mike said.

Misty stayed seated as the rest filed out. She stared at Jack, her eyes narrowing. When the room was empty, she asked, "Why are you taking Rena on your team?"

"Because I plan to be the first one down the stairs," he said. "You have the experience needed to help the rookie telepath. I won't have that kind of time." He pulled Misty into his arms. "I'm counting on you to make sure she doesn't panic. I'm going to need both telepaths on their game. Putting Mindspell with you and Cap, I'll know she'll have the guidance and the confidence to get through the fight."

She smiled. "I thought you may have some other deep, dark reason for taking the gorgeous red-head instead of me."

He cupped her cheek. "I do. If you're with me, I'll worry about you." He held up his hand, stopping the protest he knew was coming. "I know you can take care of yourself. It won't stop me from trying to protect you. I'll be scared enough for you when we go."

"And you don't think I'll worry about you every second we're apart?" she asked.

He smiled. "I know you will. That's why being on different teams is important." He ran his thumb over her cheekbone. "If I saw you get hurt, things would get ugly."

She gazed in his eyes. "I think that's the nicest thing anyone's ever said to me."

He kissed her lightly, holding her tight. "I have to go see someone. Want to come with me?"

"Like I wouldn't want to spend more time with you?" she snorted. "As if."

He laughed. "You hang out with Rena too much. You sound just like her."

Misty grinned. "Well, we are best friends. Let me grab my stuff and we'll go."

Watching her walk out, Jack knew he was going to move heaven and hell to stay with the woman who restored trust and love to his life.

Chapter Thirty-One

Misty watched the city pass by as Jack drove them out to a quiet suburban office park. Four brick buildings stood in the parking lot where he pulled up and parked in front of the farthest one from the street. He led her into the lobby and passed the directory, heading straight for the elevators. He pushed the button for the seventh floor, and they rode up in silence. Misty glanced at him. She could almost see his mind working, thinking about the upcoming mission.

The elevator stopped and he held her hand as he walked to a door, the nameplate identifying it as a lawyer's office. She was puzzled, but went in as he held the door for her.

The receptionist looked up and smiled at him. "Jack, it's great to see you again. Have a seat. Harrison's almost done."

"Thanks." He went to a leather couch and sat down, pulling Misty close to him.

Misty glanced around the reception room. It was neat, tastefully decorated, the colors light and calming. Her eyes widened as she realized the receptionist called Jack by his real name. How did he know this woman? Her leg bounced with impatience. Jack's hand rested on her thigh, stilling her nervousness with his touch, and he gave her a slight smile.

She smiled back, raising an eyebrow as he rubbed

her leg, his hand dipping just barely to the inside and back out. She moved closer to him and sighed when she felt his arm go around her shoulders.

All he has to do is touch me, and I turn into pudding. I'm such a sucker.

Ten minutes later, the door to Harrison's office opened and a large woman waddled out, followed by a thin, distinguished looking man. He went over to Jack and grabbed his hand, pulling him to his feet.

"Jack." He grabbed him in a fierce hug. "It's been way too long, boss." He stepped back. "I've gotten those merger papers you wanted. Are you here for them?"

Jack shook his head. "No, but I'll take them with me." He glanced at Misty. "Something else has come up."

"Come inside." Harrison led them into his office and shut the door. "A big something?"

Jack nodded. "Harrison, this is Misty."

"It's nice to meet you." Misty tried to speak at the same volume Jack did after catching a glimpse of a hearing aid in Harrison's ear. She looked around his office, taking in the large mahogany desk, the framed art on the walls, and the rows and rows of legal texts. On the bottom shelf, she noticed the new James Patterson novel and smiled.

"And you, miss," Harrison said, shaking her hand.

"Misty and I were married recently," Jack said.

Harrison stared intently at her. "Carol would've approved." He led the way to his desk. "I take it you want to change your will?"

"You were right to have a draft prepared." Jack hesitated. "It's time to finish what we started."

Harrison stared at him and frowned. He nodded toward Misty. "Does she know?"

Jack nodded. "She's going."

"Agent or paranormal?"

"Paranormal," Misty answered.

Harrison sat back and smiled. "Good. Keep him out of trouble, will you?"

She grinned. "I try, but trouble seems to find him."

He laughed. "I'll draw up the new will. Give me a couple of hours. I wish I was going with you, but I think I'd be more of a liability."

Jack shook his head. "I need you here where I know you're safe and doing my paperwork."

"Still don't like the pencil pusher side of the job?"

Jack grinned. "Did I ever?" He stood. "We'll be back around three."

In the elevator, Misty stared at him. "Was Harrison part of your team?"

Jack nodded. "He was my tactician. His receptionist was my sniper. That girl could pick off a target from almost any distance. She's got a gun under her desk to keep Harrison safe. He knew almost as much as I did about what was going down, back then."

The elevator bell dinged and let them out in the lobby. Outside in Jack's van, he said, "After I was sentenced, my team scattered. Harrison had his hearing damaged by a grenade, so he went back to school and got his degree. He's been my lawyer ever since I escaped."

"So, what did he mean by merger papers?" Misty asked. "And what will changes do you need to make?"

Jack stared straight ahead. "In case the worst should happen, I've made you the heir to my estate."

"What estate?" Misty frowned. "You said you were broke. Are you giving me the Chevy? If so, I want to repaint it."

He pulled over in front of a small cafe and turned to her. "I'm actually worth millions. I own several corporations and have a few smaller businesses that are doing well. Remember the house I took you to the first time we talked?"

She nodded. "That's yours, isn't it? The house, the grounds, everything. No wonder you weren't worried about the owner." She narrowed her eyes as she stared at him. "You must be the mysterious friend Amy mentioned. So, are those all the identities you have?"

"Yes, I am, and no, there're more, but it will take too long to list them all, and I'd like to have some lunch." He got out and went around to open her door. "Care to join me?"

Misty stepped out of the van and grinned at him. "You're going to take some getting used to, but it should be fun."

****

"Jack, there's a real obnoxious bastard here to see you. He kind of reminds me of you." Rena met them at the door when they returned to Challengers Headquarters. "I put him in the briefing room."

Jack grinned. "Good. He got my message."

"Who's here?" Misty asked,

"You may remember him from your apartment," Jack said.

Her eyes narrowed. "The guy who tried to bust my door apart?"

"That's him. And don't look like that. He's all right."

They headed for the briefing room and walked in to see Cyber-X leaning back in a chair, his feet propped up on the table. Jack strode over to him and shook his hand.

"Glad you could make it," he said. "You've been told why I want to hire you?"

"I was given a figure. That was serious?"

Jack nodded. "I've been told that's your usual fee, plus I added an extra twenty percent. You interested?"

"Oh yeah, I'm interested," Cyber-X said, rising to his feet. "When do we go?"

"Day after tomorrow," Jack said. "We're looking to leave before sunrise."

Cyber-X nodded. "I'll be here." He held his hand out, giving Jack a grim smile when he took it. "I've got a feeling, this time, you're going to win."

****

"Good work, everyone," Cap called out as the workout program shut down. "I think we're coming together well. Tomorrow's the real thing. Get some rest."

Everyone headed to their rooms, and Jack put his arm around Misty's shoulders and held her close. He closed the door to their room and began stripping off his weapons and armor. Misty just smiled. He pulled the rubber band from the back of his hair and scratched his head, pausing when he saw her watching him.

"What?"

She let her gaze wander over his body. "Everything you do is sexy."

He grinned at her and finished undressing. "How about you? Do you do everything sexy, too?"

"Heck, no." She ran her hands over his bare chest.

"That's your job."

He loved the feel of her hands on him. "Want to help me shower?"

She laid her head on his chest. "You have to ask?"

He removed the clothes from her, letting them pile on the floor with his, and pulled her into the bathroom. He turned on the water and shoved the curtain closed as she joined him. He lowered his head, letting the hot water hit the back of his neck.

Misty's fingers began kneading the tension out of his shoulders, and he smiled, remembering his vision of her doing exactly this. He gazed at her briefly before taking her mouth in a hungry kiss. Pulling her tightly against him, her body meshed perfectly with his. He tenderly kissed the water droplets from her face, and his hands moved down, tracing and memorizing every curve, every hollow, every inch of her.

She tilted her head back allowing him to trail hot kisses down her throat to her chest. He went lower, finally dropping to his knees as he pressed his lips to her belly. His hands ran up the back of her, holding her tight.

Misty laid her hand on top of his head. "I'll always be here for you, Jack. I will always love you."

He slowly rose then lifted her and wrapped her legs around him, turning her to the wall for support. "I love you, Misty," he whispered. "I always will."

He held her and she gripped him hard as they made love, the warm water making everything perfect.

Chapter Thirty-Two

Misty woke before Jack and lay there, gazing at him while she stroked his hair. She smiled when his eyes opened. "Good morning."

"Good morning, yourself," he said. His hold tightened on her. "Today's the day."

"I know," she said in a low voice. "Everything will work out. Trust me."

He lifted his head and placed his hand on her chest. "I do trust you."

She threaded her fingers in his hair. "We have a little time before we need to meet with the others."

He raised up, kissing her as his hands gently caressed her.

****

Jack and Misty were the last two to join the others in the briefing room. When everyone looked up, Misty was sure they knew what they'd been doing. Cyber-X stood off to the side as Misty hurried to her place next to Rena.

"Anything to eat?" Misty asked her.

Rena pushed a box of donuts and a canned soda in front of her. "Surprise! The condemned ate hardy." She grinned. "If you'd been on time, you could've had the last jelly donut." Rena waved the pastry under Misty's nose before taking a bite out of it.

Misty scowled. "You fiend!" She looked in the box

and picked out something with icing. "Sugar's sugar, and you can't beat carbonated caffeine this early in the morning."

Jack looked over the assembled heroes. "They're probably going to be expecting us."

Mindspell frowned. "How?"

"When Mike started getting his team together, someone was bound to let it slip, either accidentally or deliberately," Jack said. "There's going to be someone there that no one would suspect, and he'll report the activity to the renegade leaders."

The teams looked at each other and nodded. Jack looked up as a man in ULTRA armor came in. "Captain Starblast, your transports are here."

The captain stood. "Let's do it, people."

The heroes filed out, following the agent to the waiting vans. Misty stopped as Jack grabbed Rena's shoulder.

"Scan the drivers," he whispered. "We've come too far to get careless now."

Rena nodded. "Both are loyal to the true ULTRA and to Mike."

Misty watched the heroes head for the vans and begin to get in. "Do you sense any bad vibes at all?"

Rena shook her head. "Not yet. As soon as I do, you guys will be the first to know."

"As soon as you can, get linked with Mindspell," he said. "I'm not taking any chances this time."

She frowned. "Still pushy. Still paranoid. Glad getting married hasn't changed you." She shrugged. "But you're the fearless leader here, boss."

Jack looked at her sharply. "What?"

She grinned. "You did offer me a place on your

team the last time we did this. I thought for now, I'd call you what your team does."

Jack and Misty looked at each other and smiled. "Glad you're back to your old self, Red. And I'd be glad to have you on my team, even if you are so flippant."

"Thanks," she said, then frowned at him. "I think."

As Rena headed toward the second van, Jack and Misty climbed into the first one. He held her hand tightly as the vans pulled out and they were on their way.

****

The vans dropped off the two teams near the ULTRA building and left. Jack hurried them over to where Mike was waiting. Misty noticed the cameras all pointing away from where the agents stood.

"We'll go in here, Mike," Jack said in a low voice. "Send in some of your people to hold the hallway and to keep most of them from escaping."

Mike grasped his hand. "Good luck, Jack. I'll be waiting for your call." He saluted the former field commander.

Jack slowly returned the salute, grinning as he did so. "It's been too many years since I've done that."

He turned his gaze to the assembled agents, noticing the Grave Diggers unit scattered amongst the crowd. Mike had quietly issued them armor and weapons, and gave them the plan.

It's good to see us back where we belong, he thought. He turned and caught Rena smiling at him and knew she'd read his thoughts. She gave him a thumbs up.

He glanced down at Misty and took her hand in his.

He nodded once, then turned to the agents around him.

"I'm Jack McClennan," he said, then waited while the murmurs died down. "I have provided proof of a hidden cabal to Commander Mike Frailer. My team and I have been given permission to go in and get them."

He paused, staring at the crowd. "There may be agents of this organization among you now. All radios have been jammed. Telepathic contact will be the only means of communication."

He waited again while they talked to each other, glad to see a little bit of suspicion creep into their manners. "All personnel will follow the plan being presented now. My team and I will go in first. You will come in behind us and secure all clear levels. Trust only yourself. If you are in doubt about anyone, fire. I'll take all responsibility."

He stared at them, his eyes hard. "Remember, failure is not an option."

Jack watched his old team move out to the edges of the agents, weapons primed and ready. He gazed down at Misty. Cupping her chin, he leaned down kissing her hard. "Be careful."

"You, too." Her eyes shone with tears. "We're supposed to plan a big wedding."

Jack nodded at her and smiled, forcing himself to let her go. He turned back to the agents and smiled seeing them grin and point at him and his wife. "Let's go."

Jack opened the security door, knowing that an alarm would be triggered as soon as the key card was accepted. Well, they were probably already compromised, so it didn't really matter.

Jack led his team in first, making sure the others

waited the right amount of time before following. *"Cap, my team will take the lower floors. You clear the upper. We'll meet you on five",* he said through the mindlink.

"Understood."

Jack's team found no one on the first level they checked. They checked around them every few seconds, the only sign was the nervousness among them.

Rena turned to Jack. "You'd think they'd have some agents up here to at least let them know how big a force is coming."

"I don't like this," Jack muttered. "Rena, do you get anyone at all?"

She shook her head. "Nada. All I'm picking up is you guys. The psychic blanket around this building is intense. If I wasn't sure before, I am now. Their armor is definitely somehow patched into the psychic shield. It would be the only way I couldn't get any readings at all."

"Seems like a logical conclusion," he said.

As they descended the stairs, Rena sent a telepathic message to both teams. *"This is how it was when we came for Jack. As soon as we made it to the fifth floor, agents came from everywhere. Watch yourselves."*

As soon as Jack's team entered the fifth and final level, agents poured from the walls and attacked. Jack pulled his pistol and watched. Rena slammed the agents around with her telekinesis. From the viciousness of her attack, he could believe she'd walked the dark side.

"Keep your eyes open," Jack told the teams. *"We need to find the door to the Council's area."*

An agent broke through and swung his gauntlet blade trying to cut Jack's throat. Jack jerked back, the tip of the knife slicing open his cheek from nose to ear. He fired on the agent, killing him instantly.

"That'll look good in your wedding pictures," Rena told him.

He glanced at her. *"Thanks."*

She shrugged. *"Hey, what're friends for?"*

Jack's team continued to push down the corridor. Where the bloody hell was the damn door?

Cyber-X had pushed his way farther down the hall before he stopped and stared at the wall. "Jack, over here," he called, waving his hand in the air.

Jack blasted a path over to the mercenary. "What?"

"Look here." Cyber-X turned to fire on agents getting a little too close.

Jack activated the scanners in his eye. This was it! The door that would take him to the conclusion of this whole thing. There would be an ending at last, finally giving him the peace he craved.

Finding the trigger, he opened the door. "Pay dirt. Follow me when you're done here."

"Go!" Cyber-X shouted. "We'll see you soon."

Jack nodded and disappeared down the dark passageway.

Chapter Thirty-Three

The low light in the narrow corridor highlighted the less than perfect condition of Jack's armor. He watched the door slide shut and hesitated. He looked down the corridor and didn't like the way it curved off to the right. He glanced back at the door again. He knew he should wait for the others but started walking anyway. His grip tightened on his rifle, as the feeling of being cut off from his teammates pressed in on him.

"I should've waited," he muttered, as he listened to his muffled footsteps carrying him to the inevitable conclusion.

He slowed, spying a closed door at the end of the hallway. The scanners in his artificial eye picked up a figure and he stopped, readying his rifle.

The agent stepped into his path, raising his own weapon. "I can't let you proceed."

Jack shrugged. "You can't stop me. I'll kill you if I have to, but I am going through that door."

The agent nodded. "So be it."

He drew his sidearm, snapping off a shot, making Jack duck. In a split second, Jack aimed the rifle and squeezed the trigger. With the sonic rifle on the lowest setting, Jack knew the agent would live, but he'd have a hell of a nosebleed and ringing in his ears for at least a couple of days.

He stared down at the agent. "Stupid bastard. You

should've just moved."

Jack took a deep breath and pushed on the door. It swung inward, revealing a large room with an oval table near the far wall. A bright spotlight was the only illumination in the dark chamber. He holstered his rifle as he walked in.

"Talk about clichés," he mumbled. He walked closer to the table. "So you people are the Council."

"Yes, we are," said the man in the center.

Jack narrowed his eyes. "I know you. You were the head of ULTRA when all this went down."

The man nodded again.

"You were in on the whole bloody thing, weren't you?"

"I'm afraid I was." He glanced at Jack and smiled a little. "You were one of my best operatives. I had high hopes for you until you decided you needed to poke your nose in where it didn't belong. Then, you pushed harder, forcing us to rush things, and when things get rushed, mistakes get made. I'm sure you remember."

Jack stared at Fenmore and Harrington, catching a glimpse of Anita Haines behind them. Oh, he knew all right. His wife dead, his team on the run, and those who sold out to the very people he was trying to stop.

"It's over now," Jack said. "Surrender."

The Council leader laughed. "I don't think so. We have our own defenses to stop you."

Jack took two steps forward and was stopped by a force field surrounding him. "You realize how many times this has been used, right? Can't you even do one thing original?"

"Why, when this works just as well as it ever did?"

The Council leader walked around to the front of

the table. "We set up all those incredibly bad missions when a lot of agents didn't return. You were supposed to be one of them. That way, we wouldn't have had to take an active part in bringing you down."

Jack turned and watched agents enter the room, training their sights on him. He pulled the sword from his back holster. "Too good to get your hands dirty?"

"You were one of my favorites. I didn't want to have to hurt you."

Jack shrugged. "If you'd just waited, I would've given you everything I had. There was no need to kill my wife and hunt my team."

"You were getting too close," the leader said. "If you found out I was involved, it could've been bad."

"Where's my original evidence?" Jack asked. He nodded toward Fenmore and Harrington. "The idiot twins over there said you kept it."

The leader smiled. "Not smart enough to figure it out? It's under the ULTRA oath in the commander's office."

It couldn't have any more bloody obvious, Jack thought. He felt a familiar tugging at his mind.

"*Jack, we're here,*" Rena said. "*We'll move when you do.*"

"*Good because I'm going to bury this sword in the man in front of me in about two seconds.*"

Jack watched all the people in the room and noticed Anita slip through a concealed door. She must've detected his team and decided discretion was the better part of valor. Apparently, the Council didn't hold her loyalty any more than he did.

Jack idly spun the sword between his palms, activating its hidden ability. With a loud pop, he teleported behind the council table. "Now!" he shouted to his team.

The two teams rushed through the door, surprising the agents and taking most of them out before the renegades could react. Jack vaulted over the table, swinging the sword at the former ULTRA head, slicing a deep gouge on the man's chest. Rena and Mindspell grabbed the rest of the Council with telekinesis, holding them in their places. Fenmore and Harrington took off running through another door to their right.

"Jack, they're getting away!" Rena yelled.

Jack saw them disappear. "Bloody hell. I'm getting tired of chasing these two," he said then sprinted after them.

Captain Starblast watched Jack take off and turned to Misty. He nodded in the direction Jack left and smiled as she ran after him.

****

Misty desolidified to move faster. They'd all had a head start on her. She glanced down side hallways as she passed, stopping when she saw Fenmore cowering against a dead end.

"Don't hurt me!" he shouted, snapping off two shots in quick succession.

Misty watched the bullets pass through her. "A gun? Are you kidding me?" She walked over to him, turned solid, and knocked the gun from his hand. "I'm not Carol, Fenmore. You can't kill me like that." She hauled him to his feet. "You and Jack have unfinished business."

She smiled as fear filled his face. She let her hand go desolid, stuck it in his throat, and partially let it solidify, cutting off his air. "One weasel down, one to go."

She dragged Fenmore back to the junction, tied his hands and feet with his tie and belt, and went in search of Jack.

****

Jack backed Harrington against the wall. "What's the matter, Donald? No smart remarks to make when you know you're not walking out of here?"

Harrington raised his gun. "Stay away from me, McClennan."

Jack stepped closer. "What're you going to do? Shoot me? Try it and let's see what happens."

Harrington squeezed off a shot, but Jack dropped as second before he pulled the trigger. "I know what you're going to do before you do it."

Jack grabbed him by his jacket and rammed his fist into Harrington's stomach, letting him fall limply to the floor. He watched Harrington lay cringing at his feet and drew his pistol.

Taking deliberate aim, he said, "I don't think you're going to see a trial, Donald."

Harrington scurried away from him. "Don't, please."

"Carol and I said the same thing to you, but you didn't show us any mercy." Jack scowled at the man on the floor. "How's it feel to know the next few minutes are going to be your last?"

"Jack," said a soft voice. "Don't do it."

"Stay out of this, Misty." He stiffened his arm, cocking the gun.

She laid a hand on his arm. "I know what he did to you. I know he destroyed your life, and you're itching to end it now, but you can't."

"Why not?" he snarled, never taking his eyes from the sight. "Don't tell me it'll bring me down to his level or that everyone deserves a fair trial."

"I wasn't going to say anything like that," she said. "I was going to tell you it's a shame to waste good ammunition."

His head snapped in her direction, and he saw her smile. He turned back to Harrington and felt years of fatigue hit him all at once. The Council had ruled his past. They wouldn't take his future.

He yanked Harrington to his feet. "Let's go." Jack dragged him to where Misty had left Fenmore. Grabbing the other man's ankle, he took the two of them back to the main chamber.

Chapter Thirty-Four

Jack and Misty dragged their prisoners to the main room, making their way to where Captain Starblast was rounding up the remaining agents. The former ULTRA head was being tended to by the agency's medical team while being covered by three agents. No chances were being taken at this point. The whole ugly mess was finally coming to an end.

Jack dumped the two men at Starblast's feet. "Captain, I ask you to place these men under arrest for conspiracy, extortion, murder, treason, and black market arms dealing."

Cap gave him a tight smile. "My pleasure, field commander." He shoved Harrington and Fenmore in line with the rest of the Council members. "I still can't believe how badly we'd all been fooled. I wish I'd trusted my instincts and listened to you all those years ago."

Jack laid his hand on Starblast's shoulder and nodded. "It's over and done with, Cap. Don't let it worry you anymore."

As Captain Starblast lined the criminals up against the wall and read them their rights, Jack turned to Cyber-X. "Glad you were here to lend a hand. Now that I've paid you, are you going to call the contract closed?"

"I think so. You've got my number if you need

me."

"You don't want to be here for the epilogue?"

Cyber-X looked around and shook his head. "Nah. Too many ULTRA agents. They tend to make me a little jittery."

Jack nodded. "I understand." He shook Cyber-X's hand. "Maybe you could work as an undercover agent for Mike when everything is settled."

Cyber-X laughed. "I don't think so. I like being freelance. See you around, Renegade."

Jack watched him leave then walked to over to his teams, glad to see they weren't badly hurt. He pulled Misty into his arms. "How're you holding up, beautiful?"

She turned his head, examining the cut on his cheek. "Better than you, apparently. You getting old?"

Jack just smiled and pulled her close. "I'll never tell."

Mike entered with a squad who escorted the prisoners out. "Well done, people. The team outside is picking up the strays. I think we've finally gotten them all."

They could almost taste the relief at his words. They headed outside and Jack watched the Gravediggers doing what they did best. Council agents were bleeding, not moving, and cowering away from the team.

Just like the old days, he thought as he approached the commander. "We have to go to your office."

Mike stared at him. "Why?"

"I'll show you when we get there."

Not looking to see if the rest followed, Jack hurried into the main ULTRA building. The agents at the door aimed their weapons, but Mike waved them aside as he followed Jack up to his office. Jack took down the huge framed oath and ripped the backing off.

Papers and photos fluttered to the desk. Jack picked them up and read through the information and glanced at the pictures. He smiled grimly as he turned to Mike.

"This is it," he murmured. "This is my original evidence. This is what got a lot of good people killed." He handed it to Mike and watched the commander's face as he read through the papers.

"This is amazing. What I knew about the case didn't even scratch the surface of what they were doing. I didn't realize they were in so deep." He finally looked up, and Jack read the concern on his face. "You know what to do, Jack."

Jack nodded once and held his arms out. "I surrender myself to the custody of ULTRA."

"What are you doing?" Misty cried. "You can't just give yourself up!"

"I have to," he said quietly. "Now that Mike has the real evidence, it's only right I turn myself in. Mike said it would make things easier on me." He gazed at her. "I can't run forever."

Mike nodded to the two guards who had come in to stand quietly in the background before leading Jack away. "I'm in talks right now with a judge who specializes in these kind of cases," he told her. "There's a solution. Trust me."

"You said you were going to help him," Misty said. "How could you make him turn himself in?"

He laid his hand on her shoulder. "Everything is going to work out. I wouldn't have let him do this if I thought there wasn't a chance I could make things right."

She sank down in the chair in front of his desk. "I know. But for him to go through all this again..."

"It *will* be all right," Mike said. "I promise."

Misty watched Jack disappear down the hall and nodded. "You know, I fought against renegade agents, my best friend, and even Jack himself to prove how much I love him." She looked up at Mike. "You'd better know what you're doing."

"I do," he said and gave her a small smile.

Chapter Thirty-Five

Misty sat behind Jack and Harrison in the small courtroom and watched as Rena, in her hero persona took her place by the judge's bench. The High Court, which had been put together specifically to deal with villains, not only allowed telepaths to monitor the questioning, they depended on it.

The entire council had broken and confessed when they saw Rena standing nearby. Knowing she'd pick up any lie, they all told the truth from the beginning. The leader said he ordered the execution of Jack's team and the frame up of Jack himself. Fenmore confessed to murder. Harrington confessed to torture. And that was just the beginning of the crimes they'd committed. They were going to be locked away for the rest of their lives.

On the final day of testimony, Misty listened to Jack recount everything he'd been through. She winced every time he confessed to a new crime. Her hands shook, and she tried to keep her thoughts to herself, knowing Rena had to concentrate on the trial. A large hand covered hers. She turned and saw Captain Starblast smile at her.

Jack finished speaking and faced the small judge. Misty watched the two of them stare at each other, jumping a little when the woman finally spoke.

"Field Commander McClennan, while you've been

testifying, the other two judges have been observing you."

"I'm aware of that, Your Honor." He pointed to his left eye. "There isn't much this mechanical eye misses."

The judge narrowed her eyes. "Don't be impertinent. We will discuss this at length and let you know our decision. Until that time, you will remain in ULTRA's custody."

Misty shook as she watched Jack be led away by two armed ULTRA agents.

****

"Two days," Misty said as she paced in the living room. "Two days and the judges still haven't come to a decision."

Rena glanced at her, shook her head, and went back to the magazine in her lap.

"Do you think he's all right?" Misty stopped and looked at Rena. "There're a lot of criminals held at ULTRA who'd love to hurt him."

"Jack's a big boy," Rena said and flipped another page. "He can take care of himself."

Misty started pacing again. "Maybe I should go see him."

"Maybe you should trust Mike and stop wearing a hole in the carpet."

Misty folded her arms, staring hard at Rena. "I don't think you really care what happens to him."

"Have a little faith. That's all I ask."

Misty watched Rena flip the pages. "You know something, Red."

Rena just smiled and continued to look at the magazine.

****

Three days after his final testimony, Jack returned to the courtroom to receive his sentence. Harrison was already at the table, with papers lined up in three small stacks. Misty, Rena, Captain Starblast, and Mike Frailer were all in attendance when he was brought in and led to his lawyer. Harrison just smiled and went back to reading the middle stack as the judge looked over the papers on her desk.

"Field Commander McClennan, the other judges and I have discussed this case at length." She looked at him over her glasses. "You certainly don't do things by halves do you?"

Jack gave her a weak smile. "I've been told that on a number of occasions, Your Honor." Someone choked back a laugh, and he knew it was Rena.

The judge frowned at the assembly and continued. "We don't usually conduct trials this quickly, either. Your lawyer asked Commander Frailer to be expeditious in this situation in the public's best interest. The commander thought that was best and communicated those concerns to us."

The judge cleared her throat and shuffled through the papers again. "You were here for the outcome of the Council's trial. They won't ever be free to do this kind of thing again."

She made several notes then finally looked up, setting her glasses off to the side. She leaned forward and folded her hands on her desk. "Please rise, field commander."

Jack swallowed hard as he and Harrison slowly stood. He glanced at Misty. His future was about to be decided, and he wondered what that would mean to them. Would she be strong enough to deal with what came next? He noticed Rena pointedly not look at him, and her lips were slightly curved in a small smile. What did she know?

"I'll start with your team. You've requested they not serve any time, and you would take any penalties they incurred. So be it. Commander Frailer has asked that your team have their records expunged only if they will return to ULTRA to work for him. If they put one foot wrong, they will be dealt with."

The judge stared at him. "That only leaves you. Since this tribunal was formed, we've never had a case like yours. In light of your evidence, we've cleared you of the original charges and wish to extend our apologies to you for all you have suffered."

Jack nodded his head, unable to speak and wasn't sure if he wanted to anyway.

The judge took a deep breath. "However, new charges were filed because of the acts you committed since then. The Court has reviewed all of the evidence, and we find you guilty of the following charges." She picked up her glasses.

Jack cringed as the judge read from the long list. He frowned as the list went on and on. *I did all that?* It doesn't seem like he'd had enough time.

"Ha! I knew you didn't do things by halves," Rena said telepathically.

He sighed. *"Would you please let me concentrate?"*

The judge set her glasses off to the side again. "In spite of everything you've done, you have served the nation and the world to your utmost capabilities. If not for you and your team, I shudder to think what the Council would have continued to do." She paused and looked at Jack. "However, my personal feelings have no bearing and the High Court has no option but to sentence you as the law demands. None of us were happy with that, but Commander Frailer presented us with a solution."

Jack glanced at Mike, but couldn't see any betrayal of emotion on the commander's face. He simply rocked back and forth on his feet, looking like he didn't have a care in the world. Jack looked back at the judge when she cleared her throat.

"Commander Frailer has stated what you've been through has been more punishing than any prison sentence. We agree but that doesn't serve the public's best interest." She leaned forward. "You will be remanded to an additional fifteen years at the HighPower Federal Containment Facility."

Jack's shoulders sagged, and his heart sank as he heard a sob from Misty. Fifteen years was a long time to be away from her. How would he make it? He closed his eyes, almost missing what the judge said next.

"This time will be commuted to probation, as the crimes committed were only against the conspirators and their members. You'll only get this if you agree to the following two terms."

She held up her fingers. "The first condition is you will return to duty at ULTRA, go back to your position as field commander and begin training the new recruits coming in. For the second condition, you will report only to Commander Frailer as his special agent to be utilized as he sees fit, without question. Any violation of these terms and you will go to HighPower to serve the entire sentence, not just what remains. Understood? You may consult with your councilor before you tell me what you decide."

Jack turned to Harrison who just smiled and nodded. Misty ran to his side and he spun her around, kissing her soundly. Off to the side, he saw Mike high five with Rena. Mike had probably been working on this since the first time they talked. The fact that Rena knew didn't surprise him at all.

"I accept the court's judgment, your Honor." He pulled Misty tight against him. "It's a fair decision."

The judge smiled. "We thought you'd agree. Keep out of trouble for a few years and everything should be fine."

"Yeah, like that'll happen," Rena muttered, earning a frown from the judge.

"I'll do my best, your Honor," Jack said, pulling Misty closer to him.

The judge gathered her papers. "He's your problem now, Michael. Next time, bring me a difficult case like ChessMaster and his Network."

Mike nodded. "I'll try harder on the next one."

They left the courtroom and were besieged outside the doors by the media. Using her telekinesis, Rena pushed them back to let the small group get down the hallway. Mike stayed behind and held up his hands.

"I'll have a statement to give you in about twenty minutes. Please be patient."

Mike caught up to them. "Report to work on Monday. We'll discuss everything then, including some honeymoon time. I'll expect you in my office at eight in the morning." He thrust his hands in his pockets and walked back to the media mob whistling "Funny Valentine."

"Why do I get the feeling he's getting the most out

of this deal?" Jack asked no one in particular.

"Look at it from his point of view," Misty said. "He'd just gotten back one of the best teams in ULTRA history. He's gotten one of the top field commander back, too. He's just increased his experienced agents by almost thirty. Life now is good for him and ULTRA. Let him have his moment of smugness."

"Excuse me," Rena interrupted. "But which house are you guys going to live in?" She grinned at Misty. "He could stay with all your gorgeous teammates."

Misty frowned. "Not a chance." She turned to Jack. "I vote we take your country house."

He remembered the pictures he'd seen of Misty's teammates. "Are you sure? I could live with the scenery at Angel Haven."

Misty laughed, then instantly sobered. "No. Besides, they'll drive you nuts. I need only refer to Rena as an example."

"The country house it is," Jack said.

Rena sighed. "I'm so unloved."

****

Rena handed Misty more of her clothes from the dresser. "So, you're really leaving?"

Misty smiled at her. "We can't stay here forever. We all need our own lives."

Rena watched Misty snap the catches shut on the suitcase. "What am I going to do without you?"

Misty stopped and pulled Rena into a tight hug. "I'll still be around. You won't be alone."

"I know." Rena stepped back and looked at her friend. "He's good for you."

"I'm glad you finally think so. After all, I did have to bully you into helping me." Misty put the suitcase near the door.

Rena shrugged. "If I'd just given in, where would the challenge have been?"

Misty grinned. "I hear you."

Smiles disappeared from their faces, and they held each other once more. "You really are my best friend, Red," Misty said.

"Back at you." Rena wiped her eyes. "Well, we can't keep the big oaf waiting any longer. Grab a couple of bags and let's get you downstairs."

Misty walked down the main staircase where Jack waited for her at the bottom. They walked out to the car to begin their new life together.

And they had a big wedding to plan...when they returned from that honeymoon he'd mentioned.